PINBALL WIZARD

Michael D. Meloan
mdmeloan@gmail.com

PINBALL WIZARD

BY

Michael D. Meloan

IF
SF
publishing

This is a work of fiction. Names, characters, businesses, places, events, locales, and incidents are either the products of the author's imagination or used in a fictitious manner. Any resemblance to actual persons, living or dead, or actual events is purely coincidental.

FIRST EDITION

ISBN 978-1-7333864-8-7
Published by IF SF Publishing
San Francisco, California
www.ifsfpublishing.com

PINBALL WIZARD was originally published in Germany by Rodneys Underground Press as a German/English Edition in 2022

*Original **RUP** Cover Design by Jenz Dieckmann*
Cover Photo Collage by Dean Pasch

IF SF Publishing Edition Produced by
David Barich, San Francisco, California

PINBALL WIZARD

My father was in free fall. When he hit the pavement, a nauseating crunch shot through his body, then dreamy numbness. He sat on the sidewalk, unable to stand. His face turned ashen. Slowly he rolled over on his side and vomited into the sand. Three men who had been sunbathing on the beach carried him to the alley behind the condo to wait for an ambulance.

As I entered his room at Cedars-Sinai, he looked at me with bleary unfocused eyes.

"What happened?" I asked.

"I'm not quite sure." He paused and turned his gaze to the ceiling. "I was standing on the balcony looking out at the ocean..." Then he slowly spread his arms like wings, and his face twisted into a cracked smile. A rattling sound came from the bottom of his throat, like an engine. "I flew." There was a mad look in his eye that I had never seen before. "My heels were shattered," he said. Then he cut his eyes over at me. "Your mother is really pissed-off. I've never seen her like this." Pause. "I need to get some sleep. But I want you to bring me five Jack Daniel's miniatures the next time you come. Will you remember that?"

"I will," I replied.

I was on a business trip to Onizuka Air Force Base in Sunnyvale when he fell. My mother sounded exasperated in the voice mail message she left at my hotel. She said he lost his footing while trying to climb over the railing and drop down onto the beach. He'd seen younger men in other units do it, but he couldn't hang on and plummeted to the pavement. An orthopedic surgeon performed three hours of emergency surgery. He also had a concussion from smacking the back of his head on the sidewalk.

After leaving Cedars, I drove my old Citroën DS south on the 405 Freeway at 90 mph. By the time I reached Redondo Beach, the engine was running hot. I could smell burning oil as I hit the remote-control button. The metal mesh garage door strained and rattled as it slid sideways. Then I descended into the huge underground garage of "The Excelsior," an aging singles complex with a lap pool, two Jacuzzis, and a large cedar sauna. The elevators were lethargic and the hallways smelled of mold.

When I walked in, Chrissie threw her arms around me and planted a big wet kiss. She had moved into my apartment three weeks earlier. We met at a wild mid-summer costume party in Hermosa Beach. I was dressed as a seafaring yuppie, with a navy blazer, slacks, aviator sunglasses and Sperry Top-Siders. After we talked and drank wine for about an hour, I asked her to leave with me. A rare pea soup fog had descended on the entire beach area.

As we looked for my car, she asked, "Do you drive a Porsche?" I don't think she realized I was in costume. I told her I didn't drive a Porsche, but she came back to my place anyway.

We started making out as soon as we got inside the door. Then she peeled off her '60s micro-miniskirt, big gold-tone peace sign, and white turtleneck. But she kept the calf-high black patent leather boots. Reclining on my futon with long outstretched arms, she beckoned to me with a sly smile. I was nervous, but I fell into milky whiteness and flowing red hair.

Chrissie had green eyes and sculpted features. Even without makeup, her lips were red and full. But she had slightly buck teeth. The gradual slope of her breasts began from the upper chest, which made them seem fuller. Her inverted nipples only came out when she was aroused. She was easily aroused. The plastic marble counter-top of the bathroom sink was her favorite place to have sex. She'd sit with her back to the mirrored corner—a series of repeating images fanning out to infinity.

Once we were overcome by lust while driving around smoking a joint. We spotted a dark phone booth by the side of a gas station. She took off her panties before we got out of the car. Then we got inside the phone booth and wrestled the door shut. After making out ravenously, she hiked up her short skirt. Just as I entered her, a young boy and his mother came around the corner looking for the bathroom. The woman's jaw dropped when she saw us, then she jerked her son back around the corner with her hand over his eyes. I thought it was hilarious, but Chrissie was mortified.

For the most part, I was happy that she had moved in. There was a kind of healing power in her touch. Sometimes when I had a horrible hangover, she would gently cup the back of my neck with her hand and draw out the evil humors. I could feel it.

But there were a few negatives, and the negatives gnawed as time went by. Because of her buck teeth, there was a problem with her diction.

"How did things go 'wif' your father?" she asked.

"O.K.," I replied, "but he seems out of touch. Disoriented. A little bit psycho, to be honest. But he does have a concussion, so maybe that's to be expected."

"Come here," she said, dropping her magazine and stretching her arms in my direction. Without saying anything else, she pulled me into a perfumed jungle. There was no more talking, just slow kissing and caressing, no internal monologue. Sexual healing.

One night, we were drinking wine and hanging out. She was talking about how great Willie Nelson is, because no matter how old he gets, he never loses his mojo.

"Most guys seem pathetic as they get older, but Willie just gets cooler and cooler." Then she told me about an old-time folk singer she liked called Ramblin' Jack Elliott. She said he was the last of the traveling cowboy troubadours.

Suddenly she picked up her guitar. "Here's a song I just wrote." Then she sawed away. "Hoover was a vacuum man, sniffin' up those good time plans. Hoover's got a nose that really knows..."

When she finished, I said, "Those are good lyrics. Lighthearted and pretty clever. I'm impressed."

Her eyes suddenly filled with tears. Then she threw her arms around me.

A few days later, she played and sang for me again.

"Both Sides Now," by Joni Mitchell. But her singing was off-key, and her timing was terrible.

I interrupted. "You're off the melody on a number of those lines. Do you want me to run through it with you?"

"What do you know about music?" she snapped. "You're not even a musician!"

"I was the lead singer of The Tweezerhead Rebellion."

"And where did they play? Your parents' garage?"

"A number of garages around the neighborhood, not just my parents' garage."

"I've played in clubs," she said.

"At open mic nights."

"At least I get out there. You're so negative and derogatory. I 'fink' you like to cut women down. You probably have pent-up hostility toward your mother."

"She's a complicated self-absorbed personality. That's a fact," I said.

"I thought so."

Chrissie worked at a health food restaurant called Elysian Fields, owned by Linda, the live-in lover of Charles Bukowski. Linda had toured with The Who and lived with David Crosby on his yacht in Miami Harbor before hooking up with Bukowski. At 37, Linda was 23 years younger than Bukowski.

After a few shots of whiskey and a line of coke, Chrissie started rambling on about Alan Ginsberg, the Rainbow Gathering, the Grateful Dead, John Doe of the band X, etc. Her celebrity-obsessed prattle annoyed me and made her seem dim. But she had a certain intuitive wisdom. I had dated women with master's degrees in science, and for the most part, they bored me. Chrissie was fun, we partied together well, and the sex was instinctive and primal. I liked her bohemian vibe. But I wondered what my friends would think of her. I was so busy, I hadn't seen any of them for quite a while. My high school friend Chase owned an advertising and PR firm in Palos Verdes Estates. He was a tough critic, highly Darwinistic. I suspected he'd think I should try to find a better intellectual fit. But when I was sick and hung over, her hands had the power to heal. Things were good in our little love shack.

At 7:00 am, on my way out the door, I'd turn to look at her—red hair spilling over the black pillow and futon. She looked angelic in her sleep.

I spent the days programming computers for Directorate C, a secret information processing laboratory at the HighFrontier Consortium in El Segundo. HighFrontier was a Department of Defense funded think tank. The Directorates had names like "C" and "D" because the work was so clandestine, it couldn't even be named. Most of the time I was hunched over a flickering screen inside a sprawling facility with a flashing red light above the door. The beacon rotated like the cherry top on a police cruiser. It meant that high sensitivity data was visible, and no one could go in-or-out without securing the entire room by removing any secret information and putting it in a safe. There was rarely any conversation inside secure rooms.

My top-secret clearance was in-progress, so I had limited access to highly classified data. When I walked through a secure room, the desks had to be "shrouded." They threw billowing canvas bags over everything so that my wandering eyes wouldn't fall on any sensitive manuals or listings. I worked in a special isolation room for people in security limbo.

The software I wrote processed secret data, based on sets of rules provided by management. But I couldn't view the actual data until my upper echelon clearance came through. The intelligence data generally consisted of telemetry streams from spy satellites, telling where surface-to-air missile batteries were "lighting up" all over the globe. When missile launch sites beamed out radar signals to track aircraft, they registered hits on the satellite network. During various exercises, NATO would scramble fighters to the edges of enemy territory to make the missiles lock-on. The spy satellites detected radar emanations, then we built databases of the locations. But many surface-to-air batteries were mobile, so the scenario was fluid and could change within hours. It was a constant cat-and-mouse game.

The information was used to provide real time cockpit maps for fighter pilots to fly through a maze of threats, like a video game. I was bred for this work from the time I was a boy. All through elementary school I had built models of missiles and fighters. In early high school, I was a member of the Engineering Explorer Post, which was a recruitment vehicle for the defense industry. It was a direct transition from Boy Scouts, to Engineering Explorer, to software engineer supporting the Pentagon.

The defense establishment culture was an extension of high school. There were clubs and activities, even sports teams. During mandatory assemblies, the CEO would tell us how things were going in the executive suites on the sixth floor. We'd get information on the funding outlook for the next fiscal year, the status of major projects, and the average expected raise.

We were excused from work periodically to see animated films warning us to beware of strangers who seem unusually interested in what we do. In one scene, a swarthy character with five o'clock shadow was sitting on a barstool next to a guy wearing a HighFrontier Consortium (HF-C) badge.

The guy said, "So...tell me more about what you do at the HighFrontier Consortium." I almost started laughing, but when I looked around the room, everybody else was watching with rapt attention.

After one of the animated films, I was eating alone in the cafeteria. A tall gray-haired guy about 55 paused.

"Do you mind if I join you?" he asked.

"Please do," I said.

He set his tray down and extended his hand, "Charlie Phillips."

"Ralph Hargraves," I said as I shook it.

"Did you enjoy the film?" he asked, with a slight smirk.

I paused, wondering if I had read his expression correctly. Finally, I said, "It was so bizarre as to be almost psychedelic."

Charlie burst out laughing. "That's exactly my take. Glad you told me what you really think. Around here, that requires a leap of faith."

Charlie told me about marching in a major anti-nuclear protest where he gave an impromptu TV interview. On camera, he presented himself as "a defense industry scientist, concerned about the diabolical nature of American weapon systems." It caused a major stir within the company.

"I ran into the executive vice president in the hallway a few days later," Charlie said. "He asked me why I was working at The Consortium if I held such strong anti-war beliefs. I told him I wanted to change things from within."

"How did he react?" I asked.

"He just scowled," Charlie said. "Then continued on his way."

Even though Charlie had an undergraduate degree from the Sorbonne, and a PhD in physics from Princeton, his career was dead.

"My raises are shitty and promotions are non-existent. But I stay anyway," he said. "I can't really explain it. Maybe I feel like they need me around here."

In addition to his scientific talents, he wrote short stories and played jazz saxophone. He also wrote letters to politicians whenever a current event piqued his interest. And he had traveled to a number of war-torn regions to see what was going on first-hand.

"Major institutions are in the business of putting on gladiator shows to mollify us, so we'll keep our noses to the grindstone and continue consuming," he said.

After having lunch with Charlie a few times, and telling him that I had written some poetry, he invited me to jam after work in one of the company's conference rooms. I booked a space for "rehearsal of a technical presentation." Charlie brought his tenor sax and a high-quality tape recorder called a Nagra. He played slow jazzy sax riffs while I made up some improv verse. After four pieces, we took a break. He opened a black canvas bag containing bottles of dark Spaten beer. We drank and talked about our families. Charlie told me that his parents had been with the New York Philharmonic. His father played bassoon, and his mother played the flute.

"My father is a USC Business School professor," I told him. "He's always telling me about former students who have gone on to make huge fortunes. He says, 'You're in the computer game, why the hell haven't you gotten in on some of this big money? Show some initiative!'"

"I can hardly imagine being consumed by making money," said Charlie. "I don't see what people get out of it. After you buy cars and boats and planes, then what? You spend all your time fucking around with cars and boats and planes. When people suddenly get sick, and the end is in sight, it all seems ridiculously hollow."

"I agree."

"In Europe, they tend to have a more enlightened view. Their flavor of capitalism asks the question: What's best for the greater society? In America, capitalism asks: What's best for shareholder return? And what will most enrich an elite class of business executive? Our society encourages compulsive consumerism and locks people into inflexible work schedules, with almost no free time. That's how the capitalist machine feeds itself with endless legions of slaves, too busy to question their existence. Advertising and pop culture seal the deal by making people feel inadequate if they don't have more and more status symbols. And all the while, people are dissatisfied with their jobs, and lives in general. It's a pretty dismal landscape. But having said all that, I'm generally an optimist. It's my nature," he grinned.

After our beer break, Charlie and I jammed again. He was a wild and inventive musician.

A few days later at work, he slipped me a tape of the session. I was nervous when I left with it in my brief-case—taped media is strictly forbidden. It was a flagrant violation of the security rules. But Charlie liked to push the envelope.

A few weeks later, Charlie and I got together again for a jam in the meeting room. Afterward, he invited me to his home for more Spaten Optimators. He lived alone in a shiny silver aluminum Airstream trailer in Lawndale, a few miles east of the company. There was a portrait of J. Robert Oppenheimer on the wall. He told me that Oppenheimer was his tragic hero—a one-of-a-kind genius who had been co-opted by the US government, and eventually destroyed by the military-industrial establishment. According to Charlie, Oppenheimer represented everything we should watch out for—"the corruption of the sublime."

Charlie drove a strange tiny East German car called a Trabant P-601. The body was made of a chalky plastic compound. It was unlike anything I had seen before. I imagined it was the kind of car a Communist physicist would drive to work beneath the leaden skies of Leipzig.

As we drank Spaten, Charlie mentioned that he reserved 30% of his income for charities and political action groups. He also bragged that he didn't own a credit card.

"Someday I want to be completely off the grid," he said. "I'll move my trailer out to the Coachella Valley, set up a couple of wind turbines, battery packs, and a solar array, and I'll be nearly self-sufficient. Maybe I can arrange a barter deal with some local farmers to work on their computers in exchange for food. I won't need money at all!"

This sounded intriguing. But I couldn't imagine never going to a restaurant again, or getting on a plane, or buying anything. It was extreme, but he had a pure vision.

Charlie also told me that he routinely refused to work on Consortium projects that he found distasteful.

"So far, it's working," he said. "Though I think Lamont truly hates me. His father was an Air Force lifer, and he takes this militaristic ant farm mentality very seriously. To him, everything is about your position in the hierarchy. Sucking up to those higher on the ladder, and making it known to those below that you're in charge. That impulse is alien to me. I have absolutely no interest in it."

"I don't either," I said.

As I was leaving, I gave Charlie some snippets of poetry I'd been working on. He said he'd try to integrate them into the music, for our next jam.

There didn't seem to be any other employees at HighFrontier like Charlie Phillips. Most were archetypical engineering nerds. They wandered the halls like zombies wearing rumpled short sleeved shirts and cheap polyester slacks. With crusty coffee mugs in hand, they contemplated the dispersion of radioactive debris after a tactical nuclear strike. During lunch break, most sat in their offices with the doors closed. I remember talking to one guy who was generally regarded as an electrical engineering genius. His eyes darted back and forth, and never met mine.

Many of the scientific staff didn't shave regularly, and some had B.O. that was bad even by a man's standards. Dr. Howard Holtzendorf, a world-renowned structural mechanics expert, walked around mumbling to himself while carrying a stack of magnetic tapes. He had foul ashtray breath. His computer keyboard had to be taken apart and completely refurbished due to the drizzle of ashes falling from his dangling cigarette. He drove an Oldsmobile 442 that was full of dents and in dire need of a tune-up. If the car stumbled, he'd just rev it up and race the engine until he disappeared in a cloud of white smoke. Then he'd screech out of the parking lot. No time for automobile maintenance, that would cut into science. He pioneered the computer models that were used to design the space shuttle and a number of high potency nuclear reentry vehicles.

Another famous engineer, Dr. Nathan Nichols, invented a system response measure called the Nichols Plot, which is used all over the world. He also invented a highly unique coffee carrier. It was a 3.5-inch Plexiglas ring, with three long nylon strings attached. But I think he was the only one to ever use it. He would fill a Styrofoam cup of coffee all the way to the brim, then put it in the ring, and hang it by the strings. With this device, he could transport an absolutely topped-off cup and never spill a drop. It swung slowly like a pendulum as he walked along holding the strings between his thumb and forefinger. He got more government subsidized coffee for his money that way—one dime per cup.

All in all, HighFrontier was a pleasant place to work. Superficially, it was like a Norman Rockwell painting. They had a putting green, a shuffleboard court, and outdoor tables with colorful umbrellas. But I was starting to feel uncomfortable. I was neither a hawk nor a complete pacifist. And I couldn't claim to be a nihilist who didn't give a shit one way or the other. I was in limbo.

I dropped by Elysian Fields to visit Chrissie and have dinner. But she wasn't there. Linda said she'd left early to do an open mic at the Sweetwater Cafe. So, I sat down.

As I was about to order, a silver Jaguar XKE pulled up in front. A middle-aged guy with styled dark hair and an expensive blazer got out. He stepped inside.

"Ms. Cooper, I have a beef with you."

"There's your first mistake," Linda shot back. "We don't serve beef."

"All right, I've got a bone to pick. I brought some people by for lunch on Monday, and you were closed."

"I was sick," said Linda.

"When I'm feeling a little down, I come to work anyway. My patients depend on it."

"I'm sure they do. Now if you'll excuse me, I have customers to serve."

"I really think you need to improve your business discipline. That wasn't the first time you've been closed when I dropped by. You'll never make any money with that approach."

"I don't give a shit about money. That's your trip."

"That's everybody's trip."

"You'd better leave. You're starting to piss me off."

"You're starting to piss me off. Did you know I'm a co-owner of this building?"

"Fuck off. Am I supposed to kiss your ass because you own property?"

"No, you should kiss my ass because the taxes I pay will provide your unemployment after you go out of business."

Linda's eyes bugged out. She picked up a huge

serrated knife from the counter and ran at him. "Get out of my restaurant you goddamn fucking dentist!"

He bolted for the door and ran to his car. The engine revved and he screeched away from the curb. Linda started laughing manically.

"I can't stand him! He used to come in here and leer at a Playboy magazine as he ate lunch. If he evicts me, we can always relocate. Am I right?" she said to the people eating at the small round tables.

"Right," they said in unison, raising cups of herb tea.

One Saturday afternoon, Linda, Chrissie and I were sitting around the restaurant after closing time, blasting old Jimmy Cliff and Bob Marley records. Linda had turned off the neon sign and shut the Venetian blinds. Then she brought a huge water bong from the back, and fired it up with some Maui buds. She and Chrissie took massive hits. Thick ribbons of smoke wafted through the air. After a while, they started twirling slowly to the metronomic reggae beat. I sat on a big pillow watching them, drinking a can of Coors.

Suddenly a car pulled up to the curb and came to an abrupt halt. I caught a glimpse of a black Acura through the blinds. Someone beat on the door.

"Open up!"

Linda quickly opened it.

"Turn it down!" Bukowski bellowed. "I HATE THAT SHIT! AND PUT OUT THAT DOPE!"

"Hello Papa. I'd like you to meet Chrissie's friend, Ralph."

"Fuck Ralph," he said. "The computer dumped five poems I was working on, and I can't get them back."

"I'm sure Ralph could get them back," said Linda. "He's a computer expert."

Bukowski narrowed his eyes and looked at me with a little Indian cigarette clinched between his lips. "You're a computer expert?" he asked in a gravelly drawl.

"On a good day, I'm definitely a computer expert," I said.

"Well, I hope this is your day. Will you work for wine?"

"Sure," I replied.

Chrissie and I followed Bukowski and Linda back to his house on a hilltop in San Pedro. Bukowski led me up a narrow staircase to a tiny writing room with a view of the harbor. He had a plain wooden desk with a Mac on one side and an ancient black Underwood manual typewriter on the other.

"I still use the old Underwood," he said, "when I need inspiration."

He sat me down at the Mac, and I went to work.

"Deleted files are not really gone," I explained, "only the pointers to them have been erased. But eventually they will be overwritten."

Bukowski had the Norton Utilities on his system, and I was able to scan the hard disk and search for the titles of the poems. In a half hour, I'd retrieved four of the five poems he had dumped.

When I brought his poems up in the word processor,

he looked at me as if I had performed sorcerer's magic. Then he asked if I knew anything about probability theory. He played the horses three times a week at Santa Anita, and he'd been working on a complicated betting system for years. He was dying to run it past someone who really knew math. I told him I had taken advanced probability theory for engineers, but I didn't think it had much applicability to the track.

Bukowski and I went back downstairs to drink red wine and talk. I told him about "the hut," a plywood shed my high school friend Rickey Stanley's father had built in the back yard. It was our hangout for years.

"What the hell did you do in this hut, fag each other?" asked Bukowski.

"We'd sit around on filthy pillows with a bare light bulb hanging down, smoking cigarettes, talking about girls, and looking at porno mags. Sometimes we read your "Notes of a Dirty Old Man" column in the *LA Free Press.*"

"Sounds educational," said Bukowski, grinning. "Glad I could help."

"When we got bored with that, we trained Fritz the dachshund to masturbate. We pushed his butt down over and over against a pillow until he got into the rhythm. Once he got the hang of it, he was like a machine. As he pumped and pumped we cheered him on."

"Jesus, that's pretty sick shit," said Bukowski laughing. "You're putting me to shame."

At one point, I put one of his stubby Indian Beedis

in my mouth and narrowed my eyes.

"Listen kid," I drawled, "If you write their way, they will smash you down into a flattened turd." I nailed Bukowski's vocal delivery so perfectly that Linda was doubled up laughing.

He slowly turned and looked at me. "You're all right kid. Have you ever tried to write anything?"

"A few things," I said. "...they were all shit."

"Too bad," he said. "Try again sometime."

Bukowski drank glass after glass of expensive cabernet. His speech slowed and his consciousness seemed to recede. Linda was busy telling Chrissie a long story. When she mentioned traveling on a private jet with The Who, Bukowski cut his eye over.

"Bragging again about your days as a rock 'n' roll hooker?"

"You bastard! I was never a groupie or any of that shit! Pete Townsend and I were into the teachings of Meher Baba. It was a spiritual connection, and I was celibate at the time. I've told you that again and again."

"And when you drag your ass back to my house at 3:30 in the morning, I'm supposed to believe you've been drinking tea with the girls and discussing Meyer Bubba."

"You think every woman is a whore. You hate women. Admit it! That's why you're so obsessed with pussy and cock and all that down and dirty shit. You can't look a woman in the eye and relate to her as a human being. All you see is fishnet stockings, tits, and a hole."

"You're starting to piss me off. If it wasn't for me, I

don't know what the fuck you'd be doing. That shitty little restaurant would be out of business in a week. What would you do if you had to go out and get a real job? I guess you could make Slurpees at 7-Eleven. Or sell oranges on a freeway on-ramp."

"You're the kind of vile piece-of-shit that makes people jump off buildings or blow their brains out. You have a genius for sucking every ounce of hope and joy out of anyone around you."

"At least I have a genius for something. How many even have that?"

"You're right. I'm sure Hitler was a genius too."

"Why don't you move out? Go ahead and go! Do you think you're the only woman I can get?"

"No, I'm well aware that the lure of fame—even second-rate fame like yours—is a powerful aphrodisiac for trailer trash women."

"That's it!" Bukowski planted his foot underneath the wooden coffee table and kicked it over, launching glasses of wine into the air. "Get out of my house! You don't live here anymore! I mean it. We're through!" Bukowski and Linda stared at each other. Linda's jaw flexed rhythmically. Then he moved in close. "I mean it! LEAVE!" he screamed, spewing spittle in her face. Tears streamed down her cheeks.

She stood up and looked at me. "Get me out of here," she said.

"OK," I replied.

Linda, Chrissie, and I wandered slowly down the

long tree covered driveway and past the dense hedges and rose bushes that blocked a street view of the house. Linda started crying, and Chrissie hugged her under the orange sodium vapor streetlight.

I looked up at the second story window which was visible above the hedge. Bukowski was violently pounding the keys of his Underwood. Typing like a madman, head down, with machinegun rhythms. Completely absorbed, never bothering to glance out the window. We dropped Linda off at the Manhattan Beach home of a gay lawyer she had known for years.

When Chrissie and I got back to my apartment, there was a voicemail message from my mother. My father was back at home, and they wanted us to come by for dinner. Her voice sounded distant and flat. Chrissie lit up a joint and turned-on TV. I think the encounter at Bukowski's had rattled her. She needed something.

After the joint, she reached down and started rubbing my cock. She was coiling around me like a snake as we sat on the couch. Then she mounted my leg and started grinding her vulva into my thigh. She told me I needed to screw her again on top of the bathroom sink.

Two nights later, we arrived at my parents' condominium in Marina del Rey. My father hobbled slowly down the stairs on two canes with my mother hovering close behind. He wore a brown satin smoking jacket and had casts on both feet. My parents hadn't met Chrissie yet, and when my father caught a glimpse of her, his face lit up. He loved beautiful women. But he looked haggard and bent over—the accident had aged him fifteen years.

During dinner, he drank glass after glass of Chardonnay and began to complain that my mother was a cold fish. He told us she wasn't affectionate, and only came to see him in the hospital every other day. My mother's eye twitched as he spoke.

"Every other day doesn't sound unreasonable," I said.

"Shut up! You don't know what it's like to be stuck flat on your back wondering if you'll ever walk again," he said, eyes blazing.

"Dr. Hargraves," Chrissie interjected. "Have you ever tried aroma therapy? It can do wonders to improve your disposition. Sometimes the right smell is all you need."

My father looked at her incredulously, then burst out laughing. He laughed so long, it seemed odd. His mood instantly changed. It was like banging a shark on the nose. His attack instinct had been short-circuited. He started asking Chrissie questions about her family background.

Chrissie told us her mother had a serious case of wanderlust. They drove all over the US together when she was little. Starting out in Rhode Island, they roamed the country, moving to Florida, Texas, Oklahoma, and then Arizona. Her mother worked as a file clerk, typist, motel maid, almost anything.

"She always said that she was 'made for something bigger than this.' So, she'd quit her job, and we'd just move on. Sometimes when money ran low, we had to sleep in the car at truck stops.

Finally, my mother ended up in a mental institution and I had to go live with my aunt in Lawrence, Kansas."

Silence. "I'll get dessert," my mother said.

After dinner, we drank glasses of port on the balcony while watching the moon behind high wispy clouds.

"Lately I've been asking all my students to write about their most influential educational experience. What was that for you?" he asked me.

"That's easy—The International School when we lived in Torino, Italy."

"Why?" he asked.

"Because we were in an exotic environment, it was intense, and we learned so much. The schoolmasters pushed us to the limit. Experiences like that burn themselves into your psyche. You feel like you're really living."

"And what about you," he asked Chrissie.

"Seeing the Grateful Dead at Red Rocks in Colorado. I've never felt more connected to humanity and God than I felt during that concert."

My father exuded a puff of air. "The Grateful Dead is a rock group, right?"

"They're the greatest rock band of all time. They're more than a band, they're a community. They're a way of life! I quit my job once because my boss wouldn't give me time off to see a Dead show in Phoenix."

"I can't imagine losing a job over a rock concert, but I guess it takes all kinds," he said.

"Do you have a 10-year plan?" he asked Chrissie.

"Uh, no. Well...I plan to be a famous recording artist

in 10 years. Is that a 10-year plan?"

"No, absolutely not. A 10-year plan is about process. You have to map out a strategy, with milestones and sets of incremental goals, and ways of accomplishing those goals. You have to visualize your success every day. Feel it in your bones. It has to become part of your blood, part of your DNA."

"Wow, that makes some sense," said Chrissie thoughtfully. "I'd never really considered all that."

"I've been asking for Ralph's 10-year plan for quite some time. But he still hasn't given me one. When am I going to get that, Ralph?"

"I'm still mulling it over," I said, while conspicuously looking at my watch. "It's getting late, we need to head out."

On the way home, Chrissie talked about my father.

"At first, I thought your father was sort of a dork, a generic Mr. Businessman type. But he has some wisdom. I 'fink' you should do your 10-year plan. He might be right. If you don't know where you're going, you might end up in Bumfuck, Idaho."

"Thanks. Between the two of you, I'm certain to eventually see the light."

❋ ❋ ❋

Lamont was my boss at the HighFrontier Consortium. He was a sweaty heavy-breather with damp stains under his arms and a hanging gut. He had a dark choco-

late complexion and features that looked slightly aboriginal. Because of diabetes, his body emitted a pungent
sweet smell. He was only thirty-six, but he moved like
a much older man. Occasionally he made the rounds to
observe every member of his department. He wanted
a bird's-eye view into your mental processes. He'd sit
behind you in a chair, while you wrote computer code.

"Use a do while loop there, it would be much more
efficient! Where did you go to school?"

"USC," I said.

"Figures," he snapped. He sat for a few more minutes,
huffing and puffing with his arms folded. Finally, he said,
"You don't work very well under pressure, do you?"

Sometimes I felt like punching him. But he was
smart, I had to give him that. He had a master's in
computer science from MIT and a bachelor's in math
from Berkeley. And he liked to do real work, not just
abstract hand waving. He didn't mind getting his hands
dirty. That was a rare thing at HighFrontier.

Lamont called me into his office.

"Sit down," he said, opening his palm to one of the
chairs in front of his large steel desk.

I sat down, thinking he was going to explain why the
company had decided to let me go.

"In preparation for the NATO Autumn Exercises,
we'll be bouncing some encrypted intelligence data from
recon satellites and receiving the data directly at the
fighter squadron level. The project is called PINBALL
WIZARD. That's all I can tell you right now, due to

your security clearance. And don't repeat that name. On Wednesday, we're sending a small team to RAF Mildenhall in England. I need someone with solid experience writing real time data ingest software. Your resume says you did that at the Data Service Bureau in support of the LAPD. That's true, isn't it?"

"It is," I said.

"Would you say that you were good at it?"

"I would," I answered. My father taught me to answer every question with confidence, even if you don't know what the hell you're talking about.

"Good. Here's your travel packet—business class ticket to Heathrow, hotel reservation at a country inn called The Kittredge, and a Hertz rental. Ever driven English-style?"

"No"

"I hope you're a fast study behind the wheel. I'll be at USAF European Headquarters at Ramstein, Germany, running the other end of the test. You'll be traveling with two Program Office suits, so they'll be of no help to you in a technical sense. Professional schmoozers. I'll be on the first leg of the trip to Heathrow, then I'll hop over to Frankfurt and rent a car. Any questions?"

"Umm, am I supposed to write the data ingest software before we leave."

"No, I've already got that. You just install, debug and test. Anything else?"

"I...guess not."

"Good, meet you Wednesday at LAX at 4:30 pm,

our flight leaves at 6 pm. We arrive at Heathrow around noon the next day." His phone rang. He looked at me impatiently, indicating that I should leave.

That night, I told Chrissie I was going to England.

"Cool!" she said. "Maybe I should go 'wif' you. I've never been to Europe."

"Ummm, I'll be working the whole time. I don't think there will be a spare moment."

"I'd really like to go. I've never been outside the US."

"I'll be far from London. There's nothing to do where I'm staying. All you could do is take walks in the countryside and hang out at the pub where locals get drunk and sing."

"That sounds fun, I'll bring my guitar. You're always bragging about your frequent flyer miles. Now's your chance to use them."

"Uh, well, I guess I could do that. But I really don't think you'll enjoy it."

"I will. I'm very self-sufficient."

"O.K. I'll look into it."

I called the United Airlines frequent flyer desk and booked Chrissie's travel. Then I put together a backup disc of some data ingest code I had written for the LAPD.

❊ ❊ ❊

Chrissie and I took a cab to LAX. I bypassed a huge congested line and sailed through the tiny business class queue to check my luggage and pick up my boarding pass.

Then I had to wait for Chrissie to check her suitcase and guitar in coach. It took forever.

"Why didn't you get me a business class ticket?" she asked.

"I...didn't have enough mileage."

"You're lying. You said once that you had enough mileage to go around the world."

"Guys like to brag. You know how it is," I said.

She narrowed her eyes at me. Then we headed for the Red-Carpet Lounge. The haughty woman at the desk wouldn't let Chrissie in. No guests allowed.

"I have to go in and hang out with these guys for a few minutes. Sit down and wait right here, I'll be back soon."

"You really know how to treat a girl, don't you?"

"I know, I'm a shithead. I'm sorry."

Lamont saw me walk in and motioned for me to come over. He was wearing a baggy olive drab jump suit with cargo pockets all over it. The pockets were stuffed and bulging. The two other guys were wearing sport jackets and open collar dress shirts. One was a handsome GQ guy with a square jaw and razor cut black hair combed straight back. He thrust his hand in my direction.

"I'm Cecil," he said.

"Ralph," I replied.

The other guy was older, paunchy, and balding, with a bulbous red nose covered by spider veins. "I'm Vernon," he said as we shook hands. "What's your poison?"

"I'll have a Pinot Noir."

"Oh, sophisticated," said Vernon, as he waved to the

cocktail waitress.

After the drinks came, I mentioned that my girlfriend was with me, and the receptionist wouldn't let her in.

"I generally don't approve of bringing wives or girl-friends on trips like this," said Vernon.

"I agree. Makes it a lot harder to get some strange," said Cecil grinning.

"Let me go talk to the concierge," said Lamont. "I've got a Premier Executive card. That ought to be worth something."

Lamont got up and walked toward the lounge entrance. He looked ridiculous in that jump suit; I didn't think he'd get anywhere.

In about three minutes, he walked in with Chrissie at his side. Her short red dress and black strap pumps really showed off her legs.

"Wow, I'm impressed, padner," said Cecil, under his breath.

As they arrived, Lamont pulled a chair out for Chrissie. She sat down.

"You're so gentlemanly, you must be from the south," Chrissie said.

"I'm from Compton," said Lamont.

As we were finishing our drinks, Chrissie started talking about her music.

"I'm a singer/song writer," she announced. "The writer Charles Bukowski says I'm a talented lyricist."

"You know Charles Bukowski?" asked Lamont.

"I know him really well. I work with his girlfriend,

and I go over to their house all the time."

"I was into his poetry when I lived in a dismal dump in Cambridge. It was good to read about a guy who had a tougher grind than my grind," said Lamont.

"I've never heard of him," said Vernon.

"Me either," said Cecil.

Chrissie and Lamont started talking about Bukowski and his novel Post Office.

The statuesque concierge approached our table and said in a hushed voice that we could board any time we were ready.

The business class cabin of the 747 was almost empty, so we all spread out. I took a window seat. Lamont took a center section seat in the same row. After I hoisted my carry-on into the overhead bin, I went back to coach to check on Chrissie. It was nearly full back there, and she was in the middle seat in the center aisle of five across— the worst possible spot.

"I'm really mad about this ticket thing," she hissed.

"I said I was sorry. Jesus, this isn't a vacation for me. I've got a lot on my mind. Now I have to worry about you too. I told you I didn't think it was a good idea for you to come. But you insisted, so I gave in."

"I'm going home. You're an asshole!" She hailed a passing stewardess. "Miss, I need to get off. Right now!"

"Did you check luggage?"

"Yes."

"Then we'd have to take all the containers out and find your suitcase before we could take off. I'm sorry, but that is not going to happen. If this is a real emergency, I can help you get on the next flight back to Los Angeles as soon as we arrive in London. Otherwise, please take your seat and enjoy the flight."

I grinned slightly.

"Go back to your seat," Chrissie said. "Or I'll call a steward and tell him you're harassing me."

I shrugged and went back to business class.

After a meal and a movie, I settled into *Hunger* by Knut Hamsun. It was a story of alienation, with virtually no plot, but somehow managed to be quite engaging. Finally, the lights went off. Vernon and Cecil started snoring almost immediately. Lamont ordered bottle after bottle of Moët and Chandon miniatures. With the overhead spotlight trained on his tray, he scribbled frantically on pieces of yellow graph paper while sipping. Occasionally he rifled through various programmer references. I caught a glimpse of one—it was an Intel microprocessor assembly language guide. I went back to my book, and finally fell asleep.

I was awakened from a deep sleep by the sounds of burping and gagging. Lamont sat forward in his seat, trying to control his nausea. His hands were clenched on the dark blue United blanket in his lap. Suddenly a stream of stinking slush poured into the blanket. Then another. He frantically looked around the cabin to see if anyone was awake. Everyone else was asleep. I closed my eyes and pretended to be out. Then I cracked open my left eye and watched him wad the blanket up in a big ball and stuff it underneath the seat next to him. He went right back to scribbling on his sheets as if nothing had happened.

A few hours later, as the stewardesses were preparing to serve breakfast, Vernon complained in a loud voice that the cabin smelled rotten. The lead stewardess walked up and down the aisles sniffing the air. Lamont looked nervous when she approached his seat. But she couldn't figure out where the smell was coming from.

We ate breakfast without talking. As the trays were collected, the 747 began a long sweeping turn and started to descend. Outside the windows it was streaming white, as if we were inside an endless cloud.

I waited for Chrissie at the gate as hordes of people disembarked from coach. She had circles under her eyes and smelled of alcohol.

"How many drinks did you have?" I asked.

"Don't start on me," she said. "I'm in no mood for it."

We caught up with Lamont, who was sitting on a bench near the restroom. His forehead was beaded with sweat. He seemed lethargic and slightly confused as he asked me to come with him into the bathroom. I grabbed his arm as he got up, because he was unsteady on his feet. He pulled away and we walked into the bathroom together. When we were inside, he removed a small leather packet from his luggage. Then he handed me his carry-on bag.

"I need to inject some insulin. I'm about to hit the wall," he said, as he walked toward a stall. "God, what a hassle. I sometimes wonder if it's worth it."

"You shouldn't drink alcohol," I said. "No diabetic should."

"How I live and die is my business," he snapped. "Don't give me medical advice!"

He was quiet as he came out of the stall. But he seemed angry. I waited like a valet as he washed his face in the sink. When he had finished, he rooted around through his carry-on, then handed me a stack of hand-written pages.

"What's this?" I asked.

"That's your data ingest driver."

"I...uh, how long do we have to test it?"

"Don't worry, it'll work. Here's the Intel programmers guide. I'm off to Ramstein. The Hertz counter is just beyond where you exit from customs. Good luck." He grabbed his bag and walked out.

When Chrissie and I arrived at Hertz, Vernon and Cecil already had their keys and were waiting.

"Get in line," said Vernon impatiently.

"If you guys already have cars, why do I need one?" I asked.

"We need flexibility. If an emergency comes up, we may all need to go our separate ways."

I got in line and picked up the keys to a car reserved under my name. It was a Ford Fiesta—the smallest and flimsiest car Hertz carried. When we got to the parking lot, Vernon and Cecil each got into mid-sized Mercedes Benz sedans.

As they drove away, Chrissie said, "I would have ridden with one of those guys, if they weren't such jerk-offs. I love Benzes."

We made our way north on the M11 motorway toward Bury St. Edmunds in Suffolk. Driving on the left was not as difficult as I imagined. But I had my Fiesta pedal-to-the-metal and it would only go about 75 mph. Vernon and Cecil pulled away and disappeared into the distance.

The Kittredge was a sprawling country inn featuring a large flagstone A-frame house with a thick thatched roof. Tiny stone and mortar cottages were scattered around the large tract of land surrounding the main building. The innkeepers were a middle-aged couple who lived in the house and served three meals in their voluminous dining room. Chrissie and I checked in. The desk clerk presented us with a huge tarnished brass key that looked like something from a medieval castle. A large wrought iron weight was attached, making it impossible to put in a pocket. We were instructed to drop the key off at the front desk anytime we left, then pick it up again when we got back.

Chrissie went into the tiny bathroom to take a shower. I took off my clothes, got into bed, and fell asleep immediately. I was awakened from a knocked-out amnesic sleep by the unfamiliar double ring tones of a British telephone. At first, I had no idea where I was, or what time it was. I looked over and saw Chrissie in bed next to me. My heart raced when I couldn't figure out what was going on. I picked up the phone—it was Vernon.

"Ready to roll, soldier? We need to get over to the base and do some setup. Lamont is already on the satellite comm link, he's sending test data from Ramstein. Meet us in the lobby in 15."

"OK, I'll be there."

Chrissie slept through the call. I wrote her a note, but I didn't have a number for the base. After throwing on my clothes, I grabbed my oversized canvas briefcase and walked out. The boys were sitting in the lobby looking annoyed. We walked outside and got into Vernon's black Mercedes.

"Aren't we going to eat dinner?" I asked, as we pulled out of the parking lot.

"We already ate dinner, partner. You slept through it. There's one seating at 7:30 sharp. When it's over, it's over."

The MP at the base entrance had a sub-machine gun hanging from his shoulder. When he looked at Vernon's ID and orders, his eyes widened, then he snapped to salute and waved us through.

"Wow, that's the royal treatment," said Cecil.

"My orders give me a GS-15 ranking," said Vernon. "That's a Full Bird Colonel in the Air Force, same rank as the base commander. He'd better show me some hustle!"

We drove slowly next to the runways in the direction of the hangers and bunkers. The overcast sky was a black velvet dome. London was 80 miles away, RAF Mildenhall was dark. Two fighter-bombers sat side-by-side on parallel runways with their engines idling.

"The F-111s are about to take off," Vernon said. "Watch this."

The jets taxied slowly forward, then roared together down the runways with afterburners blazing. My chest rattled as I took a breath. The low frequency rumble was a bodily experience. When they lifted off, white-hot exhaust cones shot the air with intense flickering light. As the fighter-bombers accelerated upward at an impossibly steep angle, my heart rate ramped-up. The ripping-and-tearing shriek finally died down when the exhaust cones could barely be seen in the inky black distance.

"You gotta love that!" said Vernon. "If there's no God, at least there's the United States of America."

We drove across the flight line and parked next to a giant concrete Quonset hanger, designed to protect the F-111s from bombing raids or missile strikes. As we got out of the car and walked toward a steel door, a small female MP appeared wearing a huge pistol in a waist holster. The gun was almost as long as her thigh. A sign on the wall said: WARNING! USE OF DEADLY FORCE IS AUTHORIZED TO SECURE THIS FACILITY. We showed her our orders, then waited for our escort. A baby-faced Major enthusiastically shook our hands. He led us down a grey steel staircase that switched back three times before we reached the bottom.

"This underground facility is designed to survive a direct hit from a tactical nuclear weapon," he said.

As we were about to enter the communication center, the Major turned. "You're all crypto cleared, right?"

"No, he isn't," said Vernon.

"That's a big problem. I can't let him in."

"He's the programmer. Without him, we don't have an experiment."

"You couldn't find a programmer with a top-secret clearance?" asked the Major.

"We solve this problem all the time at home," said Cecil. "Just shroud the desks as he walks through, and keep him in his own little room. You've got a small computer room with a high speed comm link tied to a wall jack, don't you?"

"We do," said the Major.

"Then we're in business," said Vernon.

The Major sighed. "OK, let me go in and see what state the area is in. I'll be right back."

After waiting for about 10 minutes, an MP walked by. When he saw us, he stopped in his tracks. "Who the hell are you guys, and where's your escort?"

"We're contractors from..."

"Godammit. Get down on the floor, spread eagle! Now!"

Cecil and I put down our briefcases and got down on the freezing concrete. Vernon stood there, trying to unfold his GS-15 paperwork. The MP whipped out an automatic pistol and pointed it at him.

"Down on the floor. Right now!"

Vernon's hands trembled as he stuffed the orders

into his coat pocket and scrambled to the floor. The MP opened a walkie-talkie channel.

"I need backup in facility 14-A. And get me a brig transport vehicle."

A steel door opened and the Major reappeared.

"Why are these men on the floor, soldier?"

"Sir. They were without escort, sir. My orders dictate that I must detain any non-military personnel found in the facility without escort."

"You're right soldier. Thanks for not being intimidated. At ease, I'll take it from here."

The MP saluted. "Yes sir!" He turned sharply on his heel and walked away.

"You can get up now," said the Major, smirking.

We slowly got up, as a group of soldiers entered the facility. Everybody was gawking at us.

"You shouldn't have left us without an escort," said Vernon.

"Don't start giving me orders. Security on this base is serious business. I'm not sure you guys should even be here."

Vernon dusted off his sport jacket, and we all walked silently into the computer communications area. The desks were shrouded with billowing canvas bags. A Master Sergeant walked up and shook each of our hands.

"Which one is uncleared? Must be him, right? The guy with shaggy hair."

"You got it," said Vernon.

"OK, I'll be keeping an eye on you. Don't drink too

many liquids, I don't want my guys escorting you out to the can every 20 minutes."

The Major led Vernon, Cecil and me to a small windowless concrete room. The walls and floor were covered with brown seepage stains, but they had been buffed smooth and shiny. A small computer inside a wire mesh "tempest" cage sat on the desk, with a comm link plugged into the wall jack. The tempest cage prevented radio frequency emanations that sophisticated eavesdroppers might pick up from miles away.

Vernon and Cecil spread their stuff out on a small gray table against the opposite wall.

"How long do you think it will take to establish an operational data transfer capability?" asked Vernon. "We want to start testing the wireless link to the F-111 cockpits ASAP."

"Let's not jump the gun," I said. "The data transfer capability is non-trivial. I'll give you an estimate on that in a few hours."

"OK, let's get cracking," said Vernon.

I took out the sheets Lamont had given me and started typing in the microprocessor assembly language code. It was 10 handwritten pages of instructions. After I finished typing, I checked it over line by line, to make absolutely sure each keystroke was correct. Then I launched the assembler program, to scan the syntax for mistakes. Error messages came pouring down the screen. There were so many errors, the assembler scan terminated automatically with a message saying, "Error message quota exceeded." I felt a surge of heat rising up from the V-neck of my sweater. A shroud of depression descended. Vernon looked up as the computer started beeping, signaling buffer overflow because of the flood of messages.

"What's going on?" he asked.

"A few assembly errors," I said.

"A few, it looked like a thousand! Didn't you test this software at home?"

"I didn't write the code. It was given to me on this trip."

"By who?"

"Lamont"

"Goddammit!" Vernon looked at Cecil. "Get that fucking guy on the telephone."

Cecil couldn't get a line into Ramstein. Vernon called the Major and asked for a Flash Override—a transaction reserved for top Air Force brass. It kicks other callers off the line and monopolizes the transmission for as long as the call lasts. Vernon put the call on the squawk box so we could all hear.

"Why the hell didn't you test this code?" asked Vernon. His face was turning red.

"It's pretty simple stuff," said Lamont. "Hargraves is experienced with real time ingest processors. He can handle it. Also, I wanted to keep it loose, so we could react to changing requirements in real time. I wasn't sure what the line speed would be, how dirty the data would be, what the begin, and end-of-transmission markers would be. All of those attributes color your design decisions. We need to react to those eventualities as they come up."

Vernon paused. "OK, we'll give you a progress report as things develop."

Lamont hung up.

"So, is he right? Have you got this under control?" asked Vernon.

"Yes...it's under control."

Vernon looked at me suspiciously. I printed out the code and started going over it with a fine-tooth comb. As I paged back and forth through the assembly language programmer's guide, Vernon watched my every move.

Three hours later, I had the error messages down to about 20. By that time, it was 11:15 pm.

"I'm starting to get hypoglycemic," I said.

"Is that contagious?" asked Vernon.

"It means he's hungry," said Cecil.

"You should have gotten up and had dinner," said Vernon.

"I need you guys to get me some take-out food," I said.

"Take-out food is an American concept. They don't have that in the English countryside," said Vernon.

"There's a 24-hour truckstop off M11, we could get him something there," said Cecil.

"Jesus Christ. Now I'm a personal assistant to a code jockey. OK, what do you want?" asked Vernon.

"Something with chicken, fries, and maybe a salad,

if it looks decent."

"All right. Let's go," said Vernon. He raised his hand, indicating that Cecil should get up.

They grabbed their briefcases and left the room. I went back to the computer and started chipping away at the errors. I was making steady progress, but it was a mind-numbing grind. Each instruction performed a miniscule operation, like moving a small chunk of data from one memory location to another, or adding one number to another. It took scores of instructions to accomplish anything substantial. And it was so easy to make a mistake that would throw the whole process into chaos. But assembler code was fast, and that's what we needed to get constantly streaming data into the machine.

When Vernon and Cecil walked back in, I was hunched over the keyboard with my nose against the screen.

"Is he the Pinball Wizard, or the pinball?" asked Vernon with a chuckle.

"Looks like the pinball to me," said Cecil.

I ignored them, but stopped typing and turned my head.

"We found a place called Wimpy Burger that was open 24 hours. Here you go," said Cecil.

He set a cardboard box down next to the computer. Then handed me a large coffee and some cream cups.

"I don't drink coffee this late," I said.

"You'd better make an exception tonight. Do we have

an ingest driver that works yet?"

"Soon," I said, as I opened the box. It was filled with soggy vinegar-soaked fries and cold pressed chicken nuggets with a strange tan/gray color. I took a bite—it didn't taste poisonous, so I munched while I continued to debug. After a few minutes, I opened the coffee lid. Vernon gave me a thumbs-up when he saw me take a drink.

Soon after I had finished my nuggets and fries, Lamont called. Vernon put him on the box again.

"Ralph? Do you have an executable module?"

"Not yet. But I'm almost there."

"This is pretty basic stuff. If I have to fly over there, I'm going to be really pissed-off."

"No need for that," I said. "I can handle it."

"We'll keep working," said Vernon. "Over-and-out."

I went back to it. After about 40 minutes, Vernon started fidgeting as he shuffled through a pile of newspapers. He looked at his watch and sighed. Cecil had fallen asleep with his mouth open and his head tilted back. At 1:17 am, I got a clean assemble. Before saying anything, I linked it for execution. Then I started the executable module. It sat there waiting for input data from the Ethernet port—that was a good sign.

"I've got a testable module," I announced.

Cecil startled awake.

"It's about time," said Vernon. "Get Lamont on the phone."

With Lamont on the squawk box again, a file of test

data came across the satellite link. Suddenly the program aborted. The message said:

*** Data Buffer Overflow—Abort ***
Program Counter = 7FFB AF37 B094 1435

The screen filled with hexadecimal memory dumps and other diagnostic information.

"Fucking A! It aborted; we're fucked!" said Vernon. "You guys don't know what the hell you're doing!"

"Don't panic," said Lamont. "Computer work is always problematic, you know that. It's the nature of the beast. Let's approach this methodically. Ralph, what's your take?"

"My take is that the processor isn't fast enough to keep up with the data stream."

"That's right. So, we can either reduce the speed of the data stream, or optimize the program."

"We can't reduce the speed of the data stream," said Vernon. "The Air Force says that's non-negotiable."

"Then we have to optimize the program. Any ideas on that Ralph?" asked Lamont.

"A few. We can mandate that the program is constantly in memory and can't be swapped out. We can also make sure the operating system gives the program the highest priority at all times. Other than that, there's not much we can do. Assembler is the most efficient code available."

"Let's implement those ideas. I'll send you a test file across the satellite link that you can loop back over and over to simulate the data stream. Remember to set the speed correctly. I've got to ring off. Ummm...uh, I've gotta go. Talk later..."

The line went dead.

"He sounds like a basket case. Do you think he knows what he's doing?" asked Vernon.

"I think we're on the right track," I said.

I sat down and started to reconfigure the operating system to implement the optimizations.

After about 20 minutes, Vernon said, "There isn't much more Cecil and I can do to help, is there?"

"Probably not," I replied.

"Then I think we'll head on back to the hotel."

"How will I get back?"

"We'll be back tomorrow," he said.

"You mean I'm supposed to work all night, then work all day?"

"Hey buddy, this isn't my problem. You and Lamont made this bed, now you gotta lay in it."

Vernon and Cecil gathered up their newspapers and briefcases.

"If you need anything, dial 49 and a # sign, there's a 24-hour Tech Sergeant in the next room who will escort you to the can, get you coffee, whatever. Remember, don't step outside this room without an escort. Sayonara buddy boy. Good luck," said Vernon.

Then he and Cecil walked out the door.

I dove into the operating system mods. But I wasn't familiar with the configuration commands, so I frantically thumbed through the 1,000-page System Programmer's Guide that was included with the computer. It was typically flaky documentation with almost no examples of usage. In about an hour I had the operating system set up to keep the data ingest task in memory and at top priority. Then I set the port speed and routed Lamont's test file back through the software. It blew up again, with the same message and the same indecipherable stack dump. I was getting panicky. Why on earth hadn't we simulated this at home? It was madness. I was just about to call Lamont in Germany when the phone rang. It was Chrissie on the line.

"How's it going? Are you coming back to the hotel soon?"

"How did you get this number?"

"I couldn't sleep, so I went out for a walk. I ran into Hughie and Louie as they were pulling into the parking lot."

"Those jerks got tired and just left me here. The software is a mess, I can't get the program Lamont designed to run."

"I'm really sorry. It sounds horrible. Maybe we should just fly home on your credit card. You could get another job when we get back. You're always saying how hot the job market is."

"Hmmm, that's an interesting idea. Thanks for saying that. There's always a way out."

"Also...your father called the hotel. I spoke to him. He wants to know when you'll be home. He says the two of you have some business that needs attention."

"Well, if he calls again, tell him…uh, tell him I'll be home soon, and I'll call as soon as I get in. Does he think I'm on vacation?"

"His world has shrunk down to three feet around him. That's what happened to my mother. That's what happens when things turn really bad."

"Yeah…you're right. Thanks for calling, I'd better get back to it."

"OK, I'll give you something special when you get back."

"That'll motivate me," I said. "See you soon."

"OK, Bye Bye."

I sat for a few moments looking at the wall. Then I checked my watch—it was just after 3:00 am. I called Lamont's number inside the Intelligence HQ at Ramstein. No answer. I really didn't know what to do, so I started picking through the assembler code line by line, trying to analyze each individual instruction to see if it could be made faster or more efficient. After making about 15 mods, I ran the program again. It aborted.

I closed my eyes for a few minutes and tried to think of nothing. Suddenly, the door opened. A blond-haired Captain was standing there in a one-piece olive drab flight suit. He carried a helmet under his arm with the name "Snoopy" painted on the front.

"Hello Mr. Hargraves, I'm Captain Balfour. I heard you've been on a coding binge. I have a master's in computer science, so I know what that's like. How about a break? Would you like a tour of the F-111?"

I hesitated, wondering if there was anything else I could do to the software.

"OK...that sounds interesting," I said finally.

"Then let's head out."

Snoopy told the Tech Sergeant on duty that he would be escorting me to the flight line for some hardware testing. I followed him out of the communications facility, through a labyrinth of concrete passageways that finally emerged into a cavernous hanger area with four F-111 fighter-bombers inside. They were huge, with long black javelin noses, large wing spans, and sleek under wing fuel pods. Next to each pod, there was a large bomb. The Captain picked up a helmet and oxygen mask from a wall mounted set of cubby holes.

"Here, try this on," he said.

I slipped it over my head. It fit. We approached one of the planes, which was painted light gray to match the leaden European skies.

As we got close, I could see a cartoon of Snoopy wearing his Red Baron goggles painted beneath the cockpit. An aluminum stairway was positioned on either side of the plane. Captain Balfour climbed the ladder leading to the pilot's seat, on the left side.

"You'll be in the Wizzo seat," he said, "the Weapon Systems Officer."

"OK," I said, slowly climbing the stairs on the other side.

When we were seated side-by-side in the cockpit, he

reached over and helped me buckle the network of belts.

"We're not actually going to fly, are we?" I asked.

He paused, and looked around the hanger. "It's a slow night, light air traffic. And no exercises up on the board. A short run is a possibility. Are you up for it?"

"I..."

"Hesitate, my friend, and you are lost. Yes or no."

"Yes," I said.

He quickly made sure my oxygen mask was plugged in. Then he sat there flicking toggle switches, dialing rotaries, testing the ailerons, elevators, rudder, and checking in with the control tower. After he radioed for a flightline tech to remove the ladder platforms, an Airman came stumbling out from a back room. He quickly removed the platforms and the wheel blocks. Balfour shouted "Clear!", then closed the heavy gauge Plexiglas canopy. As he ignited the twin turbofans, the entire hanger echoed with thunder and flickering light. We sat for a few seconds, then slowly started to move.

The F-111's wings jittered up and down as we rolled over the undulating concrete. Then we stopped for a few moments at the end of the runway. With the brakes on, Balfour ramped up the power. The jet tensed for takeoff, like a sprinter in the blocks right before the starting gun. I heard the tower say, "F-111, one zero niner bravo, cleared for takeoff." Balfour released the brakes and pushed both throttle levers forward almost to the stops. The fanjet roar was astonishing. There was nothing but sound. Once we lifted off the runway, Balfour performed a *shit hot takeoff* with afterburners maxed out. His angle of attack was so steep it felt like we were climbing almost vertically into the night sky. I was pinned against my seat, barely able to breathe. He looked over at me and spoke through the comm system into my headset.

"You doing OK cowboy?"

I was a little woozy, but conscious. "I've never had motion sickness in my entire life."

"That's what I like to hear. Let's rock."

He gained some altitude, then rolled the wing over to set a new course. The afterburners were still on. I could see the airspeed indicator; we were already at 375 knots.

"Thought I might do some testing of the Terrain Following Radar. Hughes Aircraft developed the hardware and software. HighFrontier does some analysis and oversight of their work, right?"

"We do."

"Then I think you'll find this interesting. Simulations are good, but there's no substitute for the real thing."

Balfour started flipping toggles and dialing rotaries again. A ghostly image appeared on the CRT screen at the center of the cockpit. Terrain features could clearly be seen in the pitch darkness below.

"This is the Forward-Looking InfraRed night scope. You'll like this, the aircraft has an onboard database of satellite mapped terrain from all over Europe and the Arab world. I can tell the system to hug the landscape at just above treetop level. In that mode, it's almost impossible to pick us up on enemy radar. I'll put the TFR on computer-controlled autopilot at Mach .8. I could go supersonic, but I don't want to blow out any farmhouse windows. The base commander would have me on a spit."

Balfour engaged the system and we started to descend. Finally, we reached an altitude of about 800 feet traveling at nearly 500 knots. Terrain features streaked by on the greenish cockpit screen. It was mesmerizing and nerve wracking. As we approached an area of rolling farmlands, the system automatically took us higher to avoid the hills. It was an amazing piece of technology.

Snoopy went on talking for about 15 minutes without a break, explaining all the whiz-bang aspects of the plane's history, design, and technology.

Suddenly there was a lull. We were silent for a few minutes. Then he spoke again.

"I forgot a very important feature of the aircraft," he said. "Guess what happens if I pull this?" He pointed to a fluorescent orange metal tab dangling from the ceiling of the cockpit.

"I have no idea," I said.

"A lead foil shroud automatically unfurls over both of our heads."

"What for?"

With a fiendish grin, he said, "To protect us from the radiation fireball, after we deploy our nuclear ordnance."

He continued to grin. I think he was waiting for me to say, "Wow, bitchin'!"

After a few minutes of silence, he said, "We'll be at

the coast soon. This will be an interesting area to shake out the TFR." Seconds later we flew into a massive zero visibility fog bank. Outside the cockpit, it was velvet darkness punctuated by a diffused white flash every time the powerful wing tip strobes fired. The countryside below continued rushing by on the green CRT screen in the cockpit.

"We're in Scotland now. We'll be at the northern coastal fjords in about 10 minutes. I think you'll like this," he said.

The ground images on the CRT had become rocky and complex. I felt the plane start to descend.

"The system is taking us right down into the canyon structure of one of the fjords. That's how fine the terrain mapping technology is," he said.

As I glanced over to the right, one of the wingtip strobes flashed. I caught a snapshot of the craggy canyon wall, which lingered for a split second in my retina. My heart raced. The F-111 descended again.

"We're almost to the ocean. The system is taking us down nearly to sea level," he said.

Just as Balfour said this, we emerged from the fog bank into clear sky. A crescent moon was near the horizon straight ahead. It created a faint shimmering column of light across the Atlantic. As the jet headed toward the ocean, our speed increased. My breathing was fast and shallow.

"Believe the system. Let it work, it can fly the aircraft better than any pilot," said Balfour, seemingly to himself.

My heart pounded out of my chest. It looked like we were 50 feet above the water. Suddenly Balfour grabbed the stick and pulled back, shoving the thrusters to near max. The airframe shuddered violently, which I knew meant that we were near stall speed where he had little control. We climbed hard away from the ocean and picked up velocity. An electronic voice said, "TFR disengaged. Manual on."

Balfour said nothing for a few moments as we flew. I could see that he was rattled and taking deep breaths to regain his composure.

"I think the system bounced radar off the ocean bottom, not the surface. A glitch in the transition between land and sea." He paused and took another breath. "I have to admit...that was close." Then suddenly he was angry. "Goddammit. Who is the HighFrontier director assigned to Hughes?! My commanding officer will want to talk to him about this."

"I'll get that for you, as soon as my program office guys come in," I said.

Balfour said nothing else as we flew back to Mildenhall. A deep indigo was forming in the east as we landed. I looked at my watch. It was 4:45 am.

"Jump out of the plane as soon as we taxi into the hanger. I'd be toast if my CO found out I gave you a ride."

"OK," I said. "...thanks for the demo."

"Check," he said.

Balfour said nothing else to me. After the flight-line Airman had wheeled up the ladders, I hopped out.

The Captain made a b-line for the squadron debriefing room. I noticed the armpits of his flight suit were soaked through with sweat. I looked down at my shirt—mine were too.

Inside the hanger, I collared a flightline tech Sergeant.

"I need an escort back to the computer room in comm center A2A. I'm expecting an important phone call from the COIC at Ramstein."

"I can do that. But I should ask what you're doing in one of our jets, if you don't have proper clearances."

"My Crypto Clearance is in progress and scheduled to come through any day. I'm writing the software for PINBALL WIZARD, the threat avoidance experiment. Heard of it?"

"Sure, everybody is excited about that. You're writing it?"

"Yes"

"I'd like to hear more about how it works, when you get a chance."

"After we have a successful transmission, drop by the testbed, I'll run through it with you."

"Great, thanks," he said.

"Can we head out?" I asked.

He led me quickly back down the concrete labyrinth to the computer room. When I opened the door, the Sergeant turned on his heel and left. Vernon and Cecil were hunched over, eating from big McDonald's Styrofoam containers. Three large coffees were on the table.

"Where the hell have you been?!" asked Vernon.

"I took a break. I had reached an impasse."

"So, we're still not operational?"

"Correct," I said.

"Lamont is in the hospital at Ramstein," said Cecil.

"What happened?" I asked.

"He has an irregular heartbeat brought on by his squirrelly blood sugar. It's no wonder, he lives on alcohol and caffeine," said Vernon. "Of course, I should talk."

"How bad is his condition?" I asked.

"He'll live," said Vernon.

"Can I talk to him on the phone?"

"Definitely. I spoke to him about 20 minutes ago. He wasn't happy about being awakened, but now that he's up, you should call him right away."

"OK, let's do it," I said.

Vernon dialed the phone. He handed it to me as it was still ringing. Then he went back to his Styrofoam container of sausages and scrambled eggs. After about 10 rings, Lamont picked up the phone.

"Hello, Lamont?"

"I'm here," he said. His voice was heavy with fatigue and depression.

"How are you doing?"

"I'm OK, they've stabilized my heartbeat with some beta-blockers. How did your tests go?"

"The mods we discussed didn't do the trick."

"Are you on a squawk box right now?"

"No"

"O.K., here's what I want you to do. It's our only

chance to save this demonstration. Create a large block of memory within the data ingest program. Then write the incoming data into that area as it comes down from the satellite link. The data stream will end before you run out of memory. The test transmissions are all pretty small, I can guarantee that. If you don't write data out to the disk drive until after the transmission ends, the software will be able to keep up. It's writing to the disk that blows us out of the water. The computer can't handle that fast enough."

"Umm, that's...uh," I looked over at Vernon and Cecil—they were shoveling food into their mouths. "That's a promising interstitial strategy."

"Nice choice of words," Lamont said. "Let's just get through this test, then we'll mop it up when we get home."

"OK, I'll work on that optimization," I said.

"Thanks, I appreciate it," said Lamont.

Lamont hung up. Vernon took a big gulp of coffee.

"So, did you guys work something out?" Vernon asked.

"We've got a plan," I replied.

"Great. Eat some scrambled eggs, then get cracking."

I sat down and ate cold scrambled eggs, English muffins, and some nasty shriveled-up turkey sausage. After gulping down a black coffee, I was flying and ready to roll. I sat down at the computer and started coding like a madman. In an hour and a half, I had a new version of the ingest processor. I tested it against the stored test data, and it worked. I swiveled my chair around, Cecil was reading *The Sun* newspaper and checking out the topless "Page 3 Girl."

"I've got a version we can test with live data," I said.

"It's about fucking time," said Vernon. "I'll call the Colonel. He wants to witness any end-to-end tests."

While we waited for the Colonel to arrive, Vernon smiled at me. "That little girlfriend of yours was wandering around this morning in the fields next to the hotel. She was playing her guitar for the cows. She's a nutjob, isn't she?"

"Fuck off," I blurted. "She plays a guitar, what the hell do you do?"

Vernon was stunned. He and Cecil looked at me with their mouths hanging open. I went back to typing on the computer. A few moments later, the Colonel walked in with a small entourage of subordinate officers.

"This will be an important capability for the entire European theater," he said. "If you can demo a reliable functionality, I think we can guarantee a key role for HighFrontier in the design and implementation of the system."

"You won't be disappointed, sir," said Vernon. "This kind of bleeding edge technology is what HighFrontier is all about. Roughly 30% of our engineers have PhDs."

"I don't give a damn about that," said the Colonel. "I'm looking for innovation and reliability. I'm not so sure advanced degrees guarantee that. Some of the most creative companies in the Silicon Valley were founded by guys who had no degrees at all."

"That can work, when there's enough churn to shake things out," said Vernon. "In the defense industry, we don't have that luxury."

"You're absolutely right. The defense industry is not a free market economy. In fact, it sometimes reminds me of a Communist bureaucracy," said the Colonel. "When it comes to defense contractors, I always say, 'You can buy better quality, but you can't pay more.'"

Vernon looked perplexed, like he was trying to decipher a complicated puzzle. The Colonel glanced over at me.

"Are we ready for a test with live data?"

"We are," I said.

I dialed the data center at Ramstein, and got a comm Sergeant on the squawk box. "Hello, this is Ralph Hargraves with the HighFrontier Consortium at testbed A2A at RAF Mildenhall. I need a PINBALL WIZARD test burst, directed to MilSat channel foxtrot foxtrot seven seven, as soon as you can queue one up."

"I'll need an authorization for that—Major or above."

"You've got one soldier. This is Colonel Farnsworth, I'm the base commander."

"Sir, please key-in your Crypto ID on the phone pad."

The Colonel bent over and zipped through a long sequence of numbers. We waited for about a minute.

"Verified sir. I'll queue up the test data ASAP. It'll be coming your way in about 2 minutes."

I was starting to get shaky, and my heart felt a little

squirrelly. I hoped I wasn't going to end up like Lamont. I had taken all the diagnostic print statements out of the program, so there was no indication on screen of what was happening. But I was worried that if the Colonel or any of his underlings were really tech savvy, they might figure out that the software could only handle small bursts of data. Assuming it worked at all.

"Here comes the data," said the static-filled voice on the squawk box.

I had no way of knowing if the process was working, or not.

"That's it," said the voice again. "End of transmission."

I saw a brief blip as the activity light on the computer's disk drive flickered. I quickly checked the directory—a new file had just been written. Then I listed the first few records to the screen.

"It looks like valid intelligence data," I said. "Latitudes, longitudes, time stamps, and missile types. I can route the incoming files to your wireless system as soon as they come in. Then the data will be in your cockpits within minutes, assuming that side of the application is working properly."

"It's working properly, I validated every aspect of the tests myself," said the Colonel.

I started to get nervous. Usually high-rolling military guys didn't get down into the nuts and bolts.

"I'll modify our software to pass the data directly to your wireless data distribution application...hang on, this only requires a change of three lines of code," I said.

After a quick edit, I reassembled the software and brought it back up.

"It's now looking for incoming data constantly, and will pass anything that comes in directly to your wireless app."

"Great. Did you hear that Ramstein?" said the Colonel.

"Yes sir," said the voice on the box.

"Send us lots of bursts, I want to shake this thing out."

"Will do, sir," said the voice.

"Let's go to the planes. I want to see what the data looks like on the cockpit screens." Before the Colonel walked out, he turned to me, "Good work. I really appreciate you being here. You might end up saving a mission and the lives of the men in the cockpit."

I was speechless.

"Thanks for the opportunity to contribute, Colonel," said Vernon, jumping in.

About 15 minutes later, the phone rang. Vernon put the call on speaker.

"This is Colonel Farnsworth. We checked the cockpit data. The threats are in the database and they display on the cockpit maps. We're in business gentlemen. Congratulations!"

"That's great!" said Vernon.

The Colonel hung up.

"I was sweating bullets. If that test had failed, it

would have been a black eye for our entire company," Vernon said to Cecil.

"I agree," said Cecil. "Let's get the hell out of here. This dungeon is getting on my nerves."

They were both ignoring me. We gathered up our things and wound our way through the underground corridors. It was a long walk to Vernon's car. He had parked next to the enlisted canteen because he didn't want any Air Force brass to see his Mercedes.

As we drove, Vernon and Cecil talked about booking travel back to LAX. I mentioned that Major Balfour wanted to talk to somebody at HighFrontier about a serious software glitch in the F-111's TFR system.

"That's not my problem," said Vernon. "He knows how to get in touch with the Consortium."

The temperature had been dropping all morning. Fighter jets appeared from the gray overcast like suddenly materializing giant black birds. As we neared the Kittredge Inn, a light snow began to fall. It left no trace as it hit the ground.

We walked into the lobby and I spotted Chrissie in the adjoining pub. She was playing her guitar and singing, with a small group of men gathered around. They were hoisting pints of Guinness and enthusiastically singing along with her song about Hoover the Vacuum Man. They seemed to know the words.

"She's at it again," said Cecil laughing, as he and Vernon headed to their rooms. I walked toward the pub and ordered a pint of Harp Ale. It was 3:30 in the afternoon. I felt like I was about to have a heart attack and die on the spot—but what the hell. I drank my pint and listened to Chrissie play. At the end of one of her songs, she blew me a kiss and mouthed, "I love you."

When her set ended, she packed up her guitar and came over to the empty stool next to me. She reached up and touched the back of my neck with her warm hand.

"I was worried about you," she said.

"Thanks," I said. "It was a strange and difficult night."

"Did things work out?"

"Sort of. The English seem to like you," I said.

"I know! Maybe we should move here. Have you had any sleep at all?"

"No"

"I'll tuck you in. Let's go back to the room," she said.

When we got back to the room, the message light was on. It was a voicemail from Lamont, saying "Call me ASAP," with a German phone number.

I dialed the number and got a hotel. The front desk connected me to Lamont's room.

"How are you doing?" I asked.

"I'll survive. I want you to know that you did a great job. Thanks for coming through in the clutch."

"I'm glad it worked out," I said. "But that scheme is only good as long as the test files are relatively small. What if they send larger data transmissions? It will overflow the internal buffer we set up, and the program will eat itself. I can't predict how it will behave if that happens."

"I understand. But the file size is fixed during this

exercise, so that will never happen."

"These exercises sometimes scramble real enemy fighters," I said. "What if a pilot somehow gets bad data, and he flies too close to a surface-to-air missile battery? He could get shot down. We'd create an international incident."

"It won't happen," said Lamont. "After the exercise, I'll redesign the system to use a higher performance storage device. They'll never know. But if you tell them now, they'll pull the plug and we'll lose the contract."

I was silent.

"I'm flying to Mildenhall tomorrow morning to debrief Colonel Farnsworth," Lamont said. "You can go on home."

"OK," I replied.

Chrissie started kissing my neck. My mind was racing, but as soon as I turned my head, her warm kisses smothered everything. We made love, then I slipped into a dreamless dead sleep.

The next morning, we had a full country breakfast at the Kittredge Inn—poached eggs, toast with blueberry jam, fried potatoes, orange juice, and black tea with milk. There was a big fire in the hearth and I suddenly felt severed from the Consortium, my parents, and Los Angeles.

Chrissie smiled broadly across the table and looked into my eyes. "Let's spend the weekend in London. I can't go home without seeing it. I don't really care about all the touristy stuff, but at least I want to go out one night and hear some music."

"Yeah," I said. "Let's do that. Why not? I need a break from all of this bullshit."

I called the Consortium's travel agency. They set me up with a small B&B called the Marlborough on Argyle St. in King's Cross.

We checked out of the Kittredge, then drove south on the M11 motorway toward Heathrow. It was mid-morning on Friday and traffic was fairly light. After dropping the car off at Hertz, we loaded our luggage onto the Piccadilly underground line and finally emerged from the King's Cross/St. Pancras station.

"I've always loved cars," said Chrissie, "but if you lived here, you wouldn't even need one."

"We could have that in the US too," I said. "But then you couldn't wear your car as jewelry, or have a quiet place to pick your nose."

"Right. Thanks for that," she said.

Our B&B was a brick row house with a black wrought iron fence, half a block from the tube station. The Indian couple who ran it kept the temperature at a sweltering 88° F. The room was small, but nice. Everything was white: bedspread, walls, mini writing desk. There was a tiny washbasin in the room and a toilet down the hall. We unloaded our luggage, then hit the street. Chrissie's enthusiasm was contagious. We got back on the tube and headed to Hyde Park where we rented an old wooden rowboat and navigated the Serpentine Lake. The sky was iron gray and the trees were mostly bare—it was starkly beautiful. And even though it was miserably cold, Chrissie seemed to be taking it all in. I didn't want to disturb her mood by talking. After rowing, we walked to Hyde Park Corner and listened to madmen on small pedestals, ranting and raving through bullhorns. One guy asserted that London was like a gigantic tick, feeding on the lifeblood of the people, and would someday explode, spewing its toxic bile far and wide, polluting the entire world. He went on to proclaim that the communist experiment was not finished, and invited people to join the London District Committee of Communist Party of Great Britain.

"It's too bad we don't have something like this in LA," said Chrissie. "A place where fringy people can just get up and do their thing."

"Venice is kind of like this," I said.

"Yeah, but in LA it's all about self-aggrandizement. Everybody is trying to get famous. This is coming from a different place. It's a purer form of madness."

After wandering Hyde Park, we got on the Bakerloo Line, then stepped off almost randomly at Piccadilly Circus. The sun had gone down and huge electronic signs flashed—Sanyo, Coca-Cola, Fuji Film—big as billboards, rainbow colors throwing shadows of the pedestrians walking by.

We started power walking, trying to keep warm. Finally, we ducked into an elegant dark wood paneled pub. The toasty warm interior was inviting. We were shown to an intimate table for two in the corner. A female server in a white coat delivered menus. Chrissie studied it.

"I want to try something really English," she said.

When the server reappeared, Chrissie asked, "How is the pheasant?"

"It's rather high," the woman replied.

"Rather high? What does that mean?" asked Chrissie.

"It's been hung out."

"Hung out?"

"Yes," said the woman, with slight exasperation. "Hung out in a shed, until a bit of bacteria grows. It's what we call 'aging' here in England."

"Ok..." said Chrissie. "I think I'll have fish and chips with vinegar."

"The only way it comes," she said.

"I'll have the same," I said. "And two Newcastle Brown Ales. Thanks."

I handed her our menus and she was gone.

"I guess slightly rotten food is a UK delicacy," said Chrissie.

The fish and chips were delicious—crunchy North Sea cod and thick fries drizzled with vinegar.

As we were finishing the drinks, Chrissie said, "I read an article once in Rolling Stone that mentioned a club called The Diamond Dive. Have you ever heard of it?"

"No. What's so special about it?"

"It's all open mic, all the time," she said. "That's all they do. Over here, people are more into that."

We looked up the club address in one of the red

wooden phone booths with a gold crown insignia on top. The Diamond Dive was on Charing Cross Road, not far from our B&B.

It was nearly impossible to find. After wandering back and forth, I finally realized that the door was below street level. We walked down a steep set of stone stairs to arrive at a large wooden door painted forest green. Tarnished brass numerals marked the address. A small Diamond Dive sign was attached to the wall. It seemed almost like a residence, so I knocked. No answer, but I could hear an acoustic guitar being played. I opened the door. Dim lighting. A small stage in the corner, and the rest of the space was filled with folding chairs, tiny round tables, and a bar at the rear. Everything painted flat black. A single spotlight illuminated an earnest looking young guy sitting on a stool, playing a chrome dobro guitar. Albert King's "Born Under a Bad Sign." The quality of the vocal and the guitar work were astounding. I went to the bar and ordered two more pints of ale. Chrissie immediately approached a heavyset guy in a black tee shirt who seemed to be in charge. They talked briefly, then she sat down at the table and took a big drink.

"I got on the list," she said.

"You don't even have a guitar."

"Don't need one. They're going to let me use a Martin that belongs to the house."

The blues player ended his set with some improv slide guitar and a rousing "I'm a Man" by Muddy Waters. His voice was gravelly and soulful. As he left the stage, the crowd went wild. Chrissie gulped down her pint and asked me to buy her another. I went to the bar for two more. English ale packs a punch. The next act was a fairy princess with long flowing blond hair and renaissance clothes. She played a short set of material that Chrissie explained had originally been done by Sandy Denny of Fairport Convention. It was pleasant, but not really my thing. Nobody was doing any original songs. Chrissie was on her third pint of bitter when the MC came to the microphone.

"And now, a bit of a surprise, all the way from the beach of Los Angeleeze, Chrissie Lundquist! "

The crowd clapped enthusiastically. Chrissie got up and moved haltingly toward the stage. She was more stoop-shouldered than usual as she took her place on the stool and picked up the Martin acoustic. The spotlight was in her eyes, so she cupped her hand over her forehead and peered out at us.

"Hello, hallow," she tested the microphone while strumming the Martin a few times. It sounded slightly out of tune, so she started working on it, but finally gave up.

After a few chords, she said, "Martins have really narrow necks...I'm not used to that."

Drinks were flowing and the din of conversation picked-up.

"Play something sweetheart!" someone shouted.

"This is called 'Someone to Lay Down Beside Me' by Karla Bonoff. A really beautiful song," she mumbled.

The timing of her guitar strumming was off immediately and it still sounded slightly out of tune. Then the vocal began. It was wobbly and off-key, and this time she knew it. As the song progressed, the performance got worse. Finally, it ended. For a moment there was dead silence, then a tiny smattering of applause.

She started mumbling again, "Next...I'd like to play a song about Hoover..."

But before she could finish, a stocky guy near the front jumped up from his table with a folded bill in his hand.

"Listen luv," he said, "Here's a proposition. I'll give you this five-pound note if you stop playing right now. You can go over to the bar and get a pint!"

Chrissie burst into tears and jumped down from the stage. She ran for the exit. I got up from my seat and went after her, but she was already out the door. I ran up the steep flight of stairs and chased her down the sidewalk. She was sobbing. I put my arm around her.

"You should have hit that guy," she said.

"He looked like a pub brawler of some distinction. That could have been dangerous to my health. Besides... umm," I felt a touch of evil coming over me. "Possibly he's right. Maybe you should do something else. Not being able to carry a tune is a pretty big impediment for a singer...and your timing on guitar is abysmal. It's a lot to overcome."

She started crying again, then talked through her sobs. "Well...you don't have any talent either. You'll just be a cog in some big company until you're an old man...

then play checkers and feed pigeons when you're all bent over."

I suddenly felt my father's nasty disposition rising up. "At least I will have done something," I said. "You'll spend your whole life chasing a crazy dream, just like your mother. I hope you don't end up in a nuthouse like she did."

Chrissie struck like a tigress and clawed the side of my face, then ran down the street. I touched my cheek and looked at my hand—a smear of blood. Anger shot through me and I ran after her. Then paused and watched as she disappeared into the darkness.

❊ ❊ ❊

In the morning, we rode the Piccadilly line back out to Heathrow in silence. I used frequent flyer miles to upgrade her to business class. As soon as we were in the air, she put on headphones and hunkered down in her seat. She ordered endless refills of whiskey and water while watching movies. Then she finally passed out. The angry claw marks on my cheek had scabbed over and were throbbing the entire flight.

❊ ❊ ❊

My mother drove slowly along Pershing Drive until she reached a tiny abandoned street in Playa del Rey. It snaked up a large hillside and at the crest she killed the engine and turned off the lights. The area was once a residential neighborhood, but the houses had been razed by the city to make way for the north runway at LAX. Only cracked and weathered blacktop remained, with the curbs still intact. Tall parched weeds grew from where the houses had once stood.

From this vantage point, she could gaze down on the entire airport. The night was crystal clear and unseasonably warm. A constellation of distant jets hovered in the flat black sky; the furthest tiny landing lights were 25 miles to the east. She unwrapped a package of Benson and Hedges 100s and pulled out a cigarette. Suddenly realizing she didn't have a match, she ducked back into the car to use the lighter. She hadn't smoked a cigarette in 10 years. As she took a deep drag, a 747 was on final rollout. It lifted off like a giant lumbering beast of burden. Then it thundered into the air with frightening power. She took another puff as she watched it come toward her. The sound was deafening as it shrieked directly overhead. It was so close, she could see sooty filth on the underside, the intense rotating red beacon, and the massive landing gear clusters. As she turned her head, the jet continued climbing out over the ocean and started a slow sweeping turn toward the south. She noticed the markings, illuminated by the plane's onboard strobes—VARIG, Brazilian. Suddenly she imagined being on it—en route to Rio, never to return. No contact with her old life again. Just paint, drink in cafes, and listen to wonderful music. But this time, without a man. This time, only for herself.

After stubbing out the cigarette, she drove to a nearby gas station and stepped into a phone booth. Dropping a quarter in, she dialed.

❋ ❋ ❋

The voicemail message said that she was "thinking of me," but she left no return number. There were also four messages from my father. He sounded angry and impatient. But on the last, his tone was different—flat and monotonic. I was jetlagged, it was four am London time and I was feeling wasted. But I dialed his number. I could hear him fumbling with the phone.

"Yes," he said, tersely.

"It's me, Ralph," I said. "I'm back in LA."

"Thanks for calling," he said.

"What's going on? You sound…I don't know, you don't sound yourself."

"…Two nights ago, your mother brought me dinner in bed, then I watched some TV. After a while, I rang my bell…but there was no answer. I could sense there was something wrong. I could feel it. The place was so silent." His voice was shaky. "Then I struggled downstairs and found her note." I could hear him fumbling with paper. "It said, 'I put my life on hold when you were in graduate school. Then I put my life on hold again to raise the boys. But they don't need me anymore. And neither do you. I'm just a nurse, you can pay somebody for that. It's time for me to think about my happiness for a change. I've been living like a ghost for decades. In the long run, this will be a positive transition for you too. I can't imagine that you've been happy. We both need to move on. -Anna'" He sighed. His breathing was uneven; clearly about to cry.

"Would you like me to come over?" I asked.

After a long pause, he said, "Yes."

As I drove along the coast toward Marina del Rey, I was thinking about a dinner meeting a few months before he fell. He asked me to join him downtown at Floor Fifty, a restaurant at the top of the Bank of America tower. It was dark and hushed, with a sweeping panorama of city lights. As I approached the table, he opened his palm and beckoned me to sit down. After we ordered, he made small talk while we waited for the first course to arrive. Then he paused and stared at me, to heighten the suspense.

"I've created a family trust. It's designed to start building assets in preparation for a time when I'm no longer around."

"That sounds like a good idea," I said, not knowing quite how to react. It was a strange conversation, because he wasn't particularly old, nor was he in poor health. And he had no significant assets. But I nodded, and tried to go along with the gravity of the moment.

Then he began talking about my career. He wanted to know what I imagined my life would be like at 40, 50, and 60. I fantasized about doing something utterly different. But I wasn't quite sure what that would be. I couldn't tell him that.

Once again, he mentioned that if I wanted to get an MBA from USC, he would pay for it. I had no intention of going that route, but I didn't say so. Just thanked him and said I'd consider it. He also wanted me to write out my decade milestones and show them to him the next time we were together. I nodded. Then he quoted Benjamin Disraeli—"Action may not always bring happiness, but there is no happiness without action."

It's probably true that people who don't have a clear vision of their future never amount to much. For him, making it was everything. I knew I would never be able to explain myself or my point-of-view. I was looking for something. He sensed that we were made of different stuff. And because of that, we could never really be friends.

When I arrived at the condo, he led me upstairs to the bedroom where he was drinking bourbon and watching TV. I sat in a chair at his bedside and we watched the Tonight Show. His hand shook as he brought a shot glass to his lips. Then he made hungry sucking sounds as he sipped.

"She's a very attractive woman, well turned-out," he said. "Some man has picked her up, it happens all the time. I know her. She's not capable of doing this on her own, she's not decisive enough. There has to be a man involved." Then he suddenly twisted his body and turned his head. "Did you know this was going to happen?" His face was contorted with anger.

"I know absolutely nothing," I said. "She's never confided in me."

He stayed twisted for a second, scrutinizing me, then relaxed and fell back onto the mattress.

He flipped the TV from channel to channel—endless infomercials, disposable movies, and home shopping hostesses.

Finally, he said, "I have an idea. She's going to call you eventually. When she does, I want you to make a date for lunch. Call me immediately when it's concrete."

"What are you up to?" I asked.

"That's my business," he said. "Just do what I ask."

"All right," I said. "I'm totally jetlagged, got to get some sleep."

"Right," he said. "Go home and get some sleep." His tone was sarcastic.

I got on the 405 Freeway and drove 85 mph all the way to the South Bay curve. The Citroën's engine sounded like it was going to explode. When I got back to the apartment, Chrissie was listening to loud electronic trance music.

"Turn that off!" I said, as I walked in.

"You could say please. How's your father?"

"He's a basket case. I don't see how she could just run out on him like that. He doesn't know what hit him. She could have at least given him a chance to change."

"What good would that do? People don't really change."

"That's pretty cynical. I thought you were little miss join-hands-and-dance-to-springtime."

"I can imagine how a woman gets trapped, that's all."

"I can imagine how everybody gets trapped. I'm going to bed, before I pass out or go blind. I have to work in the morning."

I walked off to the bedroom while Chrissie poured herself a glass of chilled Chardonnay.

Before going to bed, I logged into the Consortium's secure server to check email. There was a message from Charlie Phillips, from a commercial internet provider.

"You probably haven't noticed yet. But I am no longer in the employ of the HighFrontier Consortium. Three days ago, I was debriefed by a Senior Level 5 and told that my termination was part of a system-wide downsizing. Then I was escorted from the facility. That evening, security officers boxed up my stuff and everything was delivered to my trailer. The die has been cast. But I was ready, the time was right. I've already towed my Airstream out to the Coachella Valley, which I had been planning to do, eventually. I'm just outside Palm Springs, temporarily, until I find a more permanent place to make my home. I'd like you to come out for a visit. We should go for a hike in Tahquitz Canyon. Make it soon, I may be going mobile any day.

–All the best, Charlie"

I replied immediately, "I want to visit. When should I come?"

He was obviously online and replied in seconds,

"Come right away. Can you leave tomorrow morning?"

I hesitated. Then wrote back, "Yes, I'll leave LA at about 9 AM. Be there around noon."

"Great," he replied. "I'm in the Safari Park trailer encampment, off Hwy 111, just beyond Palm Springs. See you tomorrow. –CP."

I walked out of the bedroom.

"I have to drive to Palm Springs tomorrow morning."

"What does your company do in Palm Springs?" Chrissie asked.

"Nothing. I'm going to visit a friend who was just eradicated from the Consortium. He's an interesting guy. It's important that I see him."

"Why is it important? If he just got fired, he sounds like a loser."

"So, now you're on the side of the company? I thought you hated the company."

"You're right, I do hate the company," she said. "But I don't like losers either."

I got up early to leave voicemail for Lamont, telling him that I was ill. Then I stopped by Pep Boys for two cans of Castrol 10W-40 motor oil, just in case. Before getting on the Harbor Freeway, I drove through Jack in the Box for a large coffee, three heavy creams, and a Canadian bacon fried egg sandwich. After creeping through the smoggy congested knot of the downtown interchange, I was doing a stop-and-go 25 mph heading east on the 10 freeway toward Riverside. By the time I reached Fontana, where weathered railroad boxcars jangle along right next to the freeway, the Citroën was overheating and I was getting woozy from carbon monoxide buildup. Rusty muffler. The needle was pegged on hot and it smelled like burning chemicals. While making my way over to find an off-ramp, traffic spontaneously unblocked and I was able to start driving 65. The needle gradually crept back down from the danger zone.

On the approach to Beaumont, the dirty haze of Los Angeles began to dissipate. The sun was suddenly vivid, as if the intensity had been turned up three notches. And I could see the beginning of the San Jacinto range in the distance. The sight of the towering mountains and indigo sky stirred a visceral feeling—as if a dark force field generated by Los Angeles was lifting.

I took the Citroën up to 80 mph and stayed there as I roared through the straight corridor opening up into the Coachella Valley. A finger of the mountain range extended right down to highway 111 where it splits off from the 10. The stony flatlands next to the road were arrayed with slowly spinning wind turbines on tall concrete pylons. Huge propellers peppered the arid rocky foothills on the other side of the freeway at the 62-junction going up into Joshua Tree. The bone-white blades silently churned the air.

I continued on 111 into Palm Springs. An occasional small Moroccan or Mediterranean hotel from the 1920s could be seen within the sweep of generic beige stucco. The San Jacinto Mountains loomed like a massive rock tidal wave that had jumped up from the ground in the recent scheme of geologic time. The mountain face was so close, you could drive a few blocks west from the main drag, park your car, and start climbing.

According to my map, Charlie's trailer park was on the outskirts of Palm Springs. I turned off Palm Canyon Drive onto S. Cherokee Way and drove to the end of the small paved road up against the mountains. It was a big encampment of doublewides anchored to the ground. But a small area was reserved for nomad trailers like Charlie's. I spotted his silver Airstream immediately. The Citroën was so overheated it dieseled for about 10 seconds when I turned off the engine. It was a little past noon when I knocked on his aluminum door. As he opened it, fragrant cooking smells.

"Hi, just in time for lunch," he said, smiling.

"What are we having?"

"Grilled portobello mushrooms, chopped carrots, sautéed spinach, and saffron rice."

"OK," I said.

Charlie had cleared out the center of his trailer. There were two small black cushions on the floor. He dished out a bowl from the range-top, then handed it to me with some chopsticks. I sat down and he followed. We ate for a few minutes in silence. It was tasty, seasoned with exotic spices. After lunch, he poured green tea from an iron pot into small porcelain cups. As we sipped, he finally started talking.

"I want to take you on a trek into the mountains this afternoon," he said. "We're going into Tahquitz Canyon, a mysterious spot."

"Umm, what are we going to do there?"

"Hunt for power," he said.

"What kind of power?"

"The kind of power Lamont wouldn't understand."
I laughed.

"But before we go up there, we need to meditate.
Tahquitz has a resident evil spirit. Our intuitive capacities need to be sharpened, in case we encounter it."
Charlie had a glint in his eye.

"OK, whatever you say. Who am I to toy with an evil
spirit?"

"Good. Have you ever meditated before?"

"A little. Not too successfully."

"I've been meditating for 25 years and I still feel like a
novice. But it's really just about turning off the chattering
internal monologue and focusing attention. There are
many different techniques to help accomplish that goal,
but the goal is always the same."

"And what happens if you accomplish it?"

"Clarity, intuition, inner peace. And if you do
enough yoga, you can learn to blow yourself."

My mind skipped a beat, then we laughed uproariously.

Charlie gathered up our dirty dishes, washed them
quickly in the stainless-steel sink, then came back to his
cushion on the floor.

"So, let's go about 30 minutes. I'll start off with some
instruction, then we'll do the rest in silence. Sit with your

legs folded, back straight, head level. Close your eyes and gaze at a point in the middle distance. Clear your mind as much as possible. Start counting your breaths, 1-2-3-4 in, pause, then 1-2-3-4 out. If your attention wanders, bring it back again and again. Keep going for clarity—no clutter, no chatter. That's about it."

Thoughts about sex with Chrissie surfaced from time to time, then I was finally able to shut it down, and I saw a blue haze in the middle of my visual field. That was new. Meditating with Charlie created a heightened experience, I was in his slipstream. When I heard him start to stir, I opened my eyes. He smiled.

"Did anything happen?"

"Yeah, something."

"Good. Hopefully we're ready for the mountain."

"You don't take this evil spirit business seriously, do you?"

"Well, yes and no. What I've learned over the years is that science is just a model—a set of theories. Those theories work pretty damn well, but they're always in flux, always being refined, revised, and sometimes even redesigned. Who knows where we'll be in 100 years, or 500 years. So, I try to keep an open mind."

Charlie slowly stood up and stretched his arms and legs. Then he picked up a canvas shoulder bag and gestured toward the door. "Shall we head out?"

As we walked toward the parking lot, Charlie said, "My Trabant is a little under the weather, getting parts is murder. You'll have to drive."

We got in the Citroën and headed toward downtown Palm Springs on Palm Canyon Drive. When we reached Mesquite Ave., Charlie told me to turn west toward the mountain. The peaks were so near and so steep that the light was already starting to wane. I killed the engine and we gazed at the giant rocky cleft of Tahquitz. The outcroppings were incredibly jagged, not yet rounded by the wear and tear of time.

"There it is," said Charlie. "I love this place. It's one of my favorite spots on the planet." He opened the door and grabbed his canvas shoulder bag from the back seat. "We need to get started."

He was on the march, across a rocky flat pan toward the cleft. I followed, walking quickly to catch up. Charlie wore a black tee shirt, black Maui board shorts, light-weight hiking boots, Ray-Ban Aviators, and a beige broad brimmed hat. Even though it was winter, the sun was hot. He moved with long strides, like a much younger man. In about fifteen minutes, we reached the mouth of the canyon. Huge boulders were scattered everywhere as if they'd fallen from the sky. A clearly visible footpath snaked up into the canyon. As we continued, Charlie navigated back and forth across the narrow canyon floor, climbing large rocks and jumping from boulder to boulder to avoid the stream running through the bottom. He got into a rhythm. Like a mountain goat, as if in sync with a spirited piece of music. Never missing a beat.

The complexity and size of the canyon became more apparent as we navigated the serpentine trail. About half way up, Charlie suggested a break. We sat on a huge flat rock and gazed at the steep walls. Ten thousand Cicadas droned like electronic chanting that emanated from every direction at once.

"This is the place where the witch of Tahquitz supposedly lives. She guards the canyon from right here. When the sun is lower, you can see the outline of an old crone on the canyon wall. That's one of the manifestations of her spirit."

"I don't feel any danger," I said. "Or any negative vibes."

"Maybe that's because we meditated before we came up. We're cloaked with positive energy."

"On the other hand, if you don't believe in any of that, maybe it ceases to exist," I said.

"It's interesting you would say that. I've been thinking about that exact concept lately, as it relates to some kind of grand theological design," said Charlie. "Consciousness and the realm of spirit may be intrinsically linked through intent. As conscious beings focus intent on spiritual pursuits, the reservoir of spiritual energy expands. And this reservoir, in turn, feeds back into consciousness, creating feelings of peace, harmony, and transcendence. The two realms are symbiotic."

"So, without us, God doesn't exist?"

"In my view, that's right," said Charlie. "The character and power of the spiritual realm relies on conscious beings exercising their will to create positive or negative energy through intent. The system gains momentum and becomes more than the sum of its parts, if sufficient numbers of people engage in transcendent pursuits, such as mediation, yoga, and prayer. It's like a constant feed-back loop. When there's more positive energy going in, the spirit realm feeds back to the realm of consciousness, and creates an environment more conducive to positive experiences."

"Interesting," I said. "So, what about the notion of the spiritual realm intervening directly in the affairs of man? In your scheme, I guess that can't happen."

"Quantum mechanics teaches that reality tends to be fuzzy. In other words, things are not necessarily this way or that. I think occasionally, the spirit realm can interact with the material world. Many people have had expe-riences of synchronicity—an unusual encounter that seems particularly fraught with significance. Or a series of unlikely events that seem amazingly interconnected. But the human brain is programmed by nature to look for and recognize patterns, so maybe it's just our hunger for meaning within random events. I'm not sure. But some-times people who are dying have visitations in hospital rooms by a stranger who offers peace and comfort, and nobody can figure out who the visitor was. There are all sorts of stories like that. So, who the hell knows? The truth is, dark matter, dark energy, gravity, everything is up for grabs. There are still many mysteries. Einstein said, 'Not everything that counts can be counted, and not everything that can be counted counts.'"

"Einstein was the man," I said.

Charlie and I sat in silence for a few minutes, gazing at the canyon walls and listening to the cicadas. Then we continued walking up the canyon. As we neared the waterfall, the boulders grew larger and we had to jump back and forth to make our way higher. Finally, we reached the end of the trail, where we faced a steep rock cliff with water cascading down from a worn V-shaped formation in the rocks high above. The falls emptied onto a huge pointed boulder and formed beautiful pools below filled with rocks of various sizes and shapes. If the water hadn't been so cold, it would have been the perfect spot for a swim. We each found a large rock and sat down. Charlie took a pouch of granola and nuts out of his canvas shoulder bag and started eating, then he handed it to me. We sat for a long time and listened to the water rushing down from above.

"Have you ever been married, Charlie?" I asked, breaking the silence.

"Yes. To Pilar. For about 8 years," he replied.

"What happened?"

"We had a values gap of sizable proportions. It was there from the very beginning, but love and lust obscured it. I suppose we both thought we could meet in the middle. But the chasm was too big." He paused. "She had been a model in Madrid, and moved to New York around the time I was finishing my PhD at Princeton. I met her in a bar in Manhattan. She was an autodidact intellectual, and seemed impressed by my academic credentials. I was impressed by her style—she was intense, fiery, and bright. We traveled all over the world together. Made love and fought in Morocco, Mykonos, India, and God knows where. She was mercurial, reactive, sometimes explosive. It finally wore me out." He cut his eye over at me and smiled. "But in the end...I'm sure glad I had those experiences. There were some beautiful days and nights." He paused. "I think she believed we could ride a rocket together to greater heights than either of us could have reached alone. And she might have been right about that, but as time went on, she started to feel like I wasn't cooperating. And that's probably true. She wanted me to become a tech startup entrepreneur. She was upfront about wanting a custom-built Moorish mansion, closets full of designer clothes, and a new BMW every three years. Her dream future was all mapped out. But it wasn't happening. I wasn't making it happen. In the end, I suppose we did move a bit closer together. She started doing yoga and got off blow. And I bought a shiny aluminum Airstream...the BMW of trailers."

Charlie cut his eyes over, and we both laughed.

We sat for a few more minutes, taking in the falls. Charlie was right, there was something unique about the ambiance of Tahquitz Canyon. It hummed with invisible energy.

Suddenly he got up and I followed his lead. We walked out of the canyon in one trek, without conversation, moving from rock to boulder and taking in the smell of water, sage, dust, and the relentless waxing-and-waning sound of the cicadas.

It was almost dark by the time we got back to the car. On the return trip to Charlie's trailer, we stopped at Las Casuelas for some take-out Mexican food. When we got back to the Airstream, he dished out the pinto beans, Spanish rice, and chicken enchiladas. They were delicious. Green tea and corn chips for dessert, then Charlie broke out his sax and played some improv jazz riffs. I just listened.

There was a natural lull after Charlie finished playing.

"I need to hit the road," I said finally.

"I'm glad you were able to visit. I don't know how much longer I'll be living here. I may buy a piece of land in the Wonder Valley outside Twentynine Palms. Or I may rent a flat in Paris. But you have my new email. Ping me from time to time. We should keep in touch."

"I'll do that," I said. "Thanks for the tour of Tahquitz, and the conversation."

When I stood up, Charlie gave me a bear hug.

As I walked to the car in the pitch black, I glanced up. The sky was breathtaking—a luminous swath of Milky Way spanned the entire dome. The temperature was plunging. The Citroën liked cold weather; I could drive it fast with no fear of overheating. Instead of driving through town, I cut across Ramon Road to the 10, then got in the left lane and hammered it. In one hour, I made the Kellogg Hill in San Dimas. It was an amazingly clear night. From the crest I could see the cluster of buildings at the core of downtown LA.

＊ ＊ ＊

My office phone rang. "Sorry to call you at work, but I thought I'd have a better chance of getting you on the line," my mother said.

"Where are you? Is everything alright?"

"Everything's fine," she said.

"So, where are you living?"

"I can't tell you that right now," she replied.

"Dad thinks there's another man," I said.

Silence. "I'll tell you everything soon. Would you like to get together sometime?"

"Yes," I said. "Why don't we have lunch next week in the Marina. At the Cheesecake Factory."

"O.K. When do you want..."

"Tuesday, 12:45," I said.

"O.K." she agreed.

When I got home from work, I called my father.

"I made a lunch date with her. Tuesday at the Cheese-cake in the Marina."

"Good. That's good. Thank you for doing it," he said wearily. Then he hung up.

There was a note on the refrigerator. Bukowski had apologized to Linda and they were living together again. Chrissie was over at the house. Twenty minutes later, the phone rang—it was Bukowski.

"Listen baby," he said in a slow drawl. "I've got these two broads over here driving me crazy. They're singing and dancing. I can't work, I can't even fucking think. So, you might as well come over too. They're decorating the Christmas tree. I need another man around to dissipate some of this female energy."

I felt frazzled and tried to bow-out, but he wouldn't take no for an answer. Soon I was driving along Pacific Coast Highway on my way to San Pedro.

When I arrived at the house, Linda and Chrissie were whirling, throwing tinsel on the tree, and drinking eggnog laced with 101 proof Wild Turkey. Bukowski was watching a video tape of Sugar Ray Leonard and Thomas Hearns duking it out at Caesar's Palace. As I sat down on the couch, he poured me a cut-glass tumbler of Châteauneuf-du-Pape red. We talked about the horses and probability theory again. He wanted a computer program that would digest all kinds of variables and information about the jockeys, the horses, the odds, and take a shot at predicting the winner. He offered to pay me to develop a test version of the software. I told him it would be a monstrous undertaking to design a system like that. It would take a small team of code hackers about six months to produce a test version. And even then, it would produce hit-or-miss results.

"The big problem," I said, "would be to break down and quantify all the input information and process it fast enough to make the bets."

Bukowski nodded and took a puff. "It's a complicated dance," he said. "You have to watch the tote board and be open to changing your mind. You can actually see the posted odds change as the big money goes in.

Then you have to ask yourself if the big betters know something you don't. Probably they don't, but sometimes they do. So, you let it all simmer for five or ten minutes, then you walk up to the window at the last second and place your bet. It's a mixture of math and intuition. And I guess you're right, it would be hard as hell to build all that into a computer."

After the track, we switched to tales of the road. I told him about my hitchhiking trips through Arizona and New Mexico when I was in college—crashing with people along the way, sleeping in ditches, and traveling for a while with two old winos. He told stories about his bum life in Atlanta and New Orleans. After wandering the country for years during his 20s, he decided that LA was his town after all. It was where he had started out, and he finally decided it was where he belonged. He lit up a Beedi that smelled like acrid burning leaves.

"Another bottle!" he shouted.

Linda scurried into the kitchen, then returned with a fresh bottle and quickly opened it for us like a wine steward. He and I sat on the couch and drank and talked. I told him about my accident.

"When I was thirteen years old, I was doing gymnastics using a bar that screws into the door jam. It was only designed for pull-ups, but I was doing forward giants. Know what that is?"

"No," said Bukowski, disinterested.

"You sit on the bar and grab on, then spin forward, around and around. It didn't hold...I smashed my face on the concrete floor—knocked out four front teeth and broke my nose. I was unconscious for twenty minutes. It could have snapped my neck or shattered my skull if the angle had been slightly different."

"Jesus Christ, you're lucky you're not strapped into a wheelchair."

"I was in a fog at first, but then I realized it had raised my I.Q."

Bukowski laughed. "That's a new one."

"Before that I was a C student in math. But I immediately started doing better. Eventually I took graduate level courses in computer science and electrical engineering."

"That brain scramble technique didn't work for Muhammad Ali. But maybe that's what happened to me too, now that I think about it. I got hit over the head with a wine bottle when I was 23. I had never written anything decent at that point. Six months later I got my first fiction in *Story*. Maybe that's the answer," he said, breaking into a smile as he cut his slitty eyes over at me through a haze of blue smoke.

We drank wine and watched more fight videos. Bukowski was drunk. He clenched a Beedi between his teeth and flicked his plastic lighter a few times. The flame suddenly shot up like a blowtorch. His left eyebrow sizzled and crackled as he jerked his head back and growled like a wounded animal. In the shadowy light, his pockmarked face looked like Godzilla. He went for the Beedi again, and lit it up.

I looked over at Chrissie. She was sitting in a chair gazing at a life-size plastic goose illuminated from the inside by a light bulb. It looked like she was in a trance. She slowly got up and whispered in my ear that she wanted to go home.

Bukowski and I decided to take pisses together in his front yard. We stood side by side on the grass next to his avocado tree.

"I like you kid," he said, turning his head. "Not on my roses, you fuck!" He grabbed my arm to jerk the stream back into the dirt. Linda stood in the doorway laughing.

As soon as we got into the car, Chrissie looked over at me with an expression of awe and bewilderment. "He really likes you! You're the only one of Linda's friends he's ever liked. I don't understand it."

"We have something in common," I said.

"What's that?"

"We're both members of a secret society. It's sort of like the Trilateral Commission and the Bavarian Illuminati," I said.

"That's not funny. There's something strange going on in America. I 'fink' things really are being manipulated by a secret order. Don't you?"

"I can't talk about it. I'm sworn to secrecy," I said.

She looked over at me, scrutinizing me. Her head wobbled slightly.

"What are you on?" I demanded.

"You're so 'shtraight,' I don't know how I put up with you. You're such a Boy Scout."

"I'm not into the drug thing," I said.

"I know. So drop it."

When we got to the apartment, she crawled into bed and collapsed. There was a message on the answering machine—my father wanted me to come over to his condo the next day after work.

❀ ❀ ❀

He answered the door, fumbling with his canes. As I followed him up the stairs, I noticed he was moving a little faster, with more spirit. He took off his robe and got back into bed. A bottle of Jack Daniel's and a hi-ball glass full of ice sat on the nightstand.

"I've acquired something very interesting," he said.

I saw a glint of silver as he pulled it from the nightstand drawer. He deliberately kept it from my sight for a few seconds, to heighten the suspense. Then he opened his palm. It was a rectangular polished stainless-steel box, about the size of a cigarette package, with a black wire hanging down. A large magnet was attached to one side.

"This is a radio transmitter," he continued. "It sends out a homing signal that can be picked up by a scanner." He pulled open the nightstand drawer and grabbed a receiver about the size of a walkie-talkie. "The transmitter broadcasts up to four miles. You'll need to attach it to the underside of her car."

"And then what? I'm supposed to tail her like a P.I."

"No," he said. "That won't be necessary. I think I've figured out who she's living with. Do you remember Gordon McIntyre? He was married to my cousin Emily. She died about a year and a half ago from cancer. Shortly after her funeral, he invited us to dinner at the Jonathan Club on the beach in Santa Monica. Your mother was talking about it for quite a while. What a great club he belongs to, what an interesting guy he is, and on and on. He was a quarterback on the UCLA football team and was thinking about turning pro, but he went to law school instead. McIntyre had a certain look in his eye when he asked your mother onto the dance floor, I remember it. Didn't think too much about it at the time. But I believe he's our man."

"What if I don't feel right about doing this? It's pretty devious."

He took a drink of whisky. "Do you want to be in my will?"

"You'd cut me out of your will?"

"I don't know what I'd do," he said, staring blankly at the television.

I felt like telling him to fuck off. But he was under a lot of stress, and I did think she was in the wrong. Finally, I said, "O.K., I'll do it. But I'm doing it because I want to know where she is too."

"Whatever," he said, handing me the transmitter. "I've got something else I want to show you." He slowly got up and walked without his canes to the closet. Then he opened the sliding wooden doors and got out a fleshy pink life-sized inflatable doll. A sagging skimpy black negligee hung from her shoulders. Her hair was coarse black nylon string. After fluffing up a pillow against the headboard, he arranged her in the bed sitting next to him. Then he carefully adjusted her position and pulled the covers up over her legs. Her huge puckered orifice mouth gave her a look of surprise as she sat there watching television.

"Well, what do you think of her?" he asked, gnashing his teeth with a leering grin.

"I...think it's on the weird side," I said.

"Well, if you'll excuse us, it's time for bed now." His eyes danced as he continued to grin fiendishly.

I tried to smile, but my face cracked into a nervous grimace. "Take care of yourself," I said. "I'll call you when the transmitter's in place."

He nodded and turned back to the TV and his hi-ball glass. I picked up the radio transmitter and the Uniden Bearcat receiver. A shroud of intense depression descended as I walked down the stairs. I wondered if he was going to lose his teaching job at USC and end up in a mental hospital.

On the drive home, the radio played a droning trance loop, while a narrator told a hallucinatory tale about a man who had crash landed his light plane in a dense jungle and was saved by an aboriginal tribe. The man was unable to communicate verbally with the people, yet he felt inexplicably at home. Finally, he decided to stay among them and not seek rescue. The story was punctuated by philosophical musings that were sometimes absurd and sometimes profound. The show changed my state, the depression lifted. I felt diamond hard as I drove beneath the powerful orange lights at the west end of LAX. The streets were strangely deserted.

Chrissie was passed out in bed when I got home. I crawled in with her, and moved up against her body. She felt clammy. As I put my arm around her, she groaned and pushed me away. I rolled over and stared up at the ceiling for a long time.

The next morning at work, I encountered Lamont in a hallway.

"How are you feeling?" I asked.

"Let's step into my office for a minute."

He looked tired and seemed especially serious. "First, I don't want anyone to know I was in the hospital."

"Fine," I said.

"Secondly, I want to thank you again for a great job. I debriefed the Colonel and he's enthusiastic about the role HighFrontier will play in their future exercises and operations."

"That's good," I said.

"I also want to make sure you don't discuss the way we worked around our data buffering problem."

"It's classified, so I won't mention it to anyone," I said.

"I knew you wouldn't, but I think it's important to state things explicitly."

"I agree."

"There's one more issue. Vernon says you told him to go fuck himself."

"I don't think I said 'go fuck yourself.' I believe I said, 'fuck you,' after he insulted my girlfriend."

"Well, I like your girlfriend. And I think Vernon is a cretin, I can't stand him. But those guys hold the purse strings. Vernon is the go-to guy for all of our overseas funding. You need to start being more pragmatic. I can get behind your career, but you've got to meet me halfway."

I was silent for a few seconds. "OK, I'll try to hold my tongue."

"That would be good."

"What did you decide to do about the buffer overflow problem in the longer haul?" I asked.

"Don't worry," he said. "I ordered some new hardware. It's under control." His phone rang. He picked it up, cupping his hand over the receiver, and said, "I have to take this."

I walked out, closing the door as I left. Then I headed to the cafeteria for a coffee. A few people had mysteriously disappeared in recent months, but nobody would talk about it. There was an undercurrent of darkness beneath the company's *Leave it to Beaver* exterior.

After working my way through a mountain of business email that had piled up while I was in England, I glanced at the time stamp in the lower right corner of the computer screen. Fourteen minutes till lunch with my mother in the Marina. As I was about to swipe my badge at the building exit, Lamont walked by.

"An Undersecretary of Defense is touring the facility around noon today. I'd like you to meet him. I've told him about our European project."

"I can't make it. I have a lunch appointment."

"This is a real opportunity to establish yourself with the company's upper management. They'll all be accompanying this guy."

"Sorry, I just can't do it."

"You're making a big mistake," he said.

"This is a family emergency," I said. "My parents are getting a divorce and my father is losing his mind. I'll be back soon," I said.

Then I turned and walked away.

I made it to the Cheesecake Factory just as my mother was gathering up her things to leave.

"I thought you'd stood me up," she said.

"I do have a job," I snapped. "I can't just leave whenever I want."

"You sound like your father," she said coolly. "Nothing is ever his fault."

We sat down and quickly ordered.

"For the first time in years, I'm not taking any Valium," she announced.

"Good. That's good," I said distractedly, thinking about the homing device. "But when are we going to find out where you're living?"

"As soon as I'm completely sure about what I'm doing, I'll let everyone know. But not until then," she said, with uncharacteristic firmness.

"That sounds like your final word."

"I'm afraid it is."

She asked about my work as we ordered.

"It's stressful as hell," I said. "But it's also fairly interesting, the pay is decent, and I travel."

"That sounds pretty good, all-in-all," she said.

The food came quickly. We talked about my brother Lee and his family in Northern California as I wolfed down chicken and shrimp jambalaya. Then we came to Chrissie.

"She's not very bright, is she?" my mother asked.

"She's not a rocket scientist."

"You aren't planning to marry her, are you?"

"I'm not marrying anybody," I said, with anger boiling up. I suddenly remembered the transmitter. "I have to make a quick call to the office. I'll be right back."

She was about to say something, but I got up and walked away. In the parking lot, I scanned the area for her Honda Accord. When I reached the car, I looked around. One of the attendants was watching me, so I took the transmitter out of my pocket and bent down to tie my shoe. A car momentarily blocked his view and I squatted down to attach the transmitter to the underside. It fell to the ground on the first try because there was so much plastic. I finally found a patch of steel and it snapped in place. As I stood up, the attendant was next to me.

"Do you mind if I ask what you were just doing?" he said, studying my face to scan-in my features.

"This is my mother's car. She mentioned that it was dripping fluids, so I thought I'd take a look. It seems fine," I said. "But keep up the good work." I turned and walked away.

When I got back to the table, my mother had already paid the bill and was putting on lipstick as she looked into the mirror of her compact.

"I have to be going," she said anxiously. "I have an important appointment."

She stood up and hugged me, then pulled away to look into my eyes. "Please try not to judge me. You have no idea what living with him has been like. He's been sucking the life out of me for years." She hugged me again, then turned and left.

I sat back down at the table and asked for a coffee refill. As I drank black coffee, a paranoid thought entered my mind. What if that little box wasn't a transmitter? What if it was a bomb? It seemed awfully large and heavy for a simple radio transmitter. But he wasn't completely insane, was he? Suddenly I noticed the time—1:25. I jumped up from the table and headed out to the parking lot.

As I walked into the lab, Lamont was on the way out.

"They were really excited about our work in Europe. I mentioned your contribution. How did lunch go?"

"Not bad. My family is...difficult."

"Mine too. Listen, I'm thinking of putting you in for an add-on clearance. We may have another mission in the next few months, this time in Ankara, Turkey. Any skeletons in your closet?"

"Not really," I said. "None that I can think of."

"Good. I had one woman wait until the polygraph test to admit that she had taken LSD about 50 times." He probed me with his gaze.

While driving out of the parking lot, I encountered Lamont in his black MGB. He could barely fit inside. His head was canted over slightly, right up against the canvas convertible top. We both hesitated for a second, then he nodded slightly and lurched forward. I could hear that distinctive English exhaust note as he pulled away.

❈ ❈ ❈

Lamont drove north on Hawthorne Blvd., then pulled into the parking lot of the Jet Strip. After paying admission, he entered the dark space. A buxom blond on stage lit up when she saw him. He sat down at a stool on the periphery and draped a 20 over the brass railing. She came right over and gave him a deep knee bend as she moved to the slow throbbing music.

"Good to see you again, darlin," she said, with a heavy southern accent.

As the woman finished her dance, the MC said, "A big round of applause for Tara, guaranteed to put a rise in your Levi's. Open your wallets gents and show her how you feel."

After collecting her bills from the brass railing, she came down from the stage and approached Lamont. He ordered a gin and tonic, then they retreated to the back of the club. They both entered a dark cubby and Lamont sat on a small bench. She stood in front of him and draped her breasts in his face while they chatted through two songs. Beads of perspiration formed on his forehead. When they were finished, he slipped her three more 20s.

After the session with Tara, he ordered chicken pot pie with peas and watched other girls dance. Then he drove back to his townhouse in North Redondo Beach. After glancing through a stack of new mail, he fell onto the sofa like dead weight, turned on the TV, and started absently flipping channels.

❋ ❋ ❋

When I got home, Chrissie was dancing and drinking again in the living room.

"I need to warn you, the phone might be tapped by the National Security Agency. They're probably going to investigate me for another high-rolling clearance. So, don't say anything about drugs, sex, The Dead, the Rainbow Gathering, The Trilateral Commission, over-throwing the US government, am I leaving anything out? They may want to send me to Ankara. On second thought, maybe you should talk about that stuff. I'm not sure I want to get involved in all this cloak-and-dagger bullshit."

"Where is Ankara?"

"In the middle of Turkey."

"Turkey sounds like just the place for you," she said laughing. "By the way, your father called. He said he got your message and wants you to come over as soon as possible."

When I arrived at the condo, my father seemed almost giddy. He was downstairs, fully dressed and ready to leave.

"I hope you brought the Bearcat scanner," he said.

I opened my briefcase. "Right here."

"Very good," he said, smiling. "I want you to drive my car. I'm afraid that crappy Citroën might break down."

As we headed south in his Mercedes S500, he gave me directions to a hillside in Playa del Rey overlooking the ocean. The area was near the north runway at LAX. He moved the antenna back and forth as he directed me to Rindge Lane—a long residential street at the rim of the neighborhood.

"I'm getting a faint signal," he said. He fidgeted nervously with the volume control on the scanner.

When we reached McIntyre's house, the signal was strong. There were no cars in the driveway, the triple garage doors were all closed. I pulled the Benz over to the curb and we sat in silence for a moment. Suddenly he opened the door and planted his cane on the sidewalk

"Wait," I yelled, "what are you going to do?"

He slammed the door and hobbled toward the front of McIntyre's house. Then he repeatedly rang the bell. The porch light came on and a robust older man with curly gray hair appeared. They were both scowling as they began to argue. I fumbled with the console switches, trying to get the passenger window down so I could hear. Suddenly my father reached out and grabbed McIntyre's shirt. McIntyre cuffed him sharply on the side of the face. The blow sent my father sprawling onto the concrete walkway. I jumped out of the car and walked quickly toward them. My mother stood behind McIntyre. She looked horrified when she saw my father on the ground. As she started toward him, McIntyre blocked her in the doorway. I lifted my father up and looked angrily at McIntyre.

"You'd better get out of here," said McIntyre. "And don't come back or I'll have you both arrested."

I could see my mother behind McIntyre. Her eyes were wild. Then they both disappeared into the shadows and the door closed.

I tried to help my father to the car, but he jerked his arm away.

We drove back to the condo in silence. He made his way upstairs, and got into bed. The inflatable doll was gone. After pouring himself a drink, he turned on the TV and began flipping channels. I sat in a chair next to the bed.

"So, what are you going to do?" I asked.

"What can I do? It looks like he's got her under some kind of macho spell. It's like she's joined a cult. I don't know if I told you this, but the guy's a divorce attorney, of all things. Talk about bad luck."

"Wow. That is bad luck."

We sat watching TV for about an hour and a half. He told me that he'd hired a cook/housekeeper to come in during the day and take care of things. Then he mentioned that he was thinking about moving to Stockholm, where a friend was a senior vice president at Volvo. There was a top marketing job waiting, he said, and the guy had even lined up a woman.

When I got back to the apartment, Chrissie was gone. I was wired and wondering if she might be partying with Linda at Elysian. So I decided to cruise by the restaurant in South Redondo. The blinds were closed when I arrived and the neon sign was off. But I could hear the throbbing beats of Bob Marley from inside. I knocked on the door. No response. I knocked again. The music came down and Linda moved close to the door.

"Who is it?" she asked.

"It's Ralph."

"Hey Ralph, hold on."

She was bubbly as she opened the door. "Come on in Ralph. Have a Red Stripe."

She opened the fridge, grabbed a bottle, and flipped the top off using a counter-mounted opener. I took a big drink.

"That's good," I said.

"Nectar of the gods, mon," she grinned. "So, what are you doing out solo?"

"I was in Marina del Rey helping my father figure out which man my mother had run off with. Then the guy almost beat my father up. Thought I was going to end up right in the middle of it. When I got home, Chrissie was gone...and here I am."

"Yes, here you are...maybe you need some tea and sympathy. A medicinal herb might help."

She grabbed the huge water pipe and a Bic lighter, and started sucking on it while running the flame around the bowl. When it glowed like a hot coal, she handed me the rubber hose. I don't usually smoke pot, it makes me feel crazy. But I already felt crazy, so why not? I took a big hit. Then one more, to finish the job. It was powerful stuff. The effect came on almost immediately. A couple of big pulls from the Red Stripe, to insulate my brain. Linda turned up the music and started moving slowly to "Get up, Stand up."

"We should go to Reggae Sunsplash," she said. "I think you'd like Jamaica."

She pulled me into the middle of the room and we danced together. "Sugar Magnolia" by The Dead came on. She started whirling with more intensity. I kept moving too. Then we danced to the slow exotic beat of "Regiment" by Eno/Byrne. After that track, the tape ended and clicked off.

We both stopped, out of breath. Then she moved in close and suddenly we were kissing. There was no moment of transition. Like a tape splice, we were passionately making out. We fell onto a couch against the wall. She was on top, kissing me, sticking her tongue in my mouth and grinding her pubis against my erect cock. Her breath was a hot swirl of pot, Beedis, and beer.

I reached underneath her peasant blouse and fondled her firm braless breasts. She made small moaning sounds. A car suddenly pulled up in front. The headlights flashed through the blinds.

"Oh my God. It's Hank! Go out the back! Go out the back!"

We both jumped up from the couch and she hustled me to the back door, opened it, and slammed it behind me. I was suddenly standing in the cold night air next to a huge trash dumpster full of rotting food. The harsh orange glare of a sodium vapor streetlight permeated everything. The world looked profoundly depressing. I was about to walk toward my car when the back door opened again.

"False alarm," said Linda. "It wasn't him. But look, you need to go. I'm sorry. Good night, OK?"

"I understand. Umm, bye." I turned and walked down the alley.

When I got back to the apartment, Chrissie was still not there. And when I woke up the next morning, the bed was empty.

Lamont dropped by my office to inform me that NSA investigators were on site. They had a few questions. He smiled and said that it would be good when I joined the top-secret club. Lamont's hand shook as he raised a large Styrofoam cup of coffee to his lips. His system seemed near collapse.

I entered a small conference room in the administration building and sat down with an investigator. He wore a cheap dark suit and had a well-groomed almost pencil line moustache. An open file folder was on the table.

"Good afternoon Mr. Hargraves," he said. "Do you know why we're here?"

"To discuss my clearance investigation, I assume."

"That's correct. Your investigation is proceeding, but there is one problem—your girlfriend, Christine Lundquist. She has two prior convictions for drug possession and she appears to be a current user. We have her under surveillance."

"Wait a minute, I didn't give permission to investigate her."

"Anyone living with you is open to scrutiny. Her behavior is an inseparable part of your security landscape. There's no way around that. Since you're not married, you could terminate the living arrangement and we would re-evaluate."

"And if I refuse?"

"Your current security clearance could also be jeopardized. And without that minimum clearance, you could not continue to work for the Consortium." The agent looked at me with no expression. Then he added, "You have one month to make a decision."

He stood up, indicating that the meeting was over.

Chrissie was back in the apartment when I got home from work. She wouldn't tell me where she had been. I asked what kind of downers she'd been using, and she matter-of-factly told me they were Quaaludes she got from a doctor Linda knew.

"I like pills," she said. "I like pot, I like alcohol, and I like sex. So, what are you going to do, have me burned at the stake?"

"I don't know what I'm going to do," I said.

She went to the refrigerator and poured herself a Chardonnay. Then she took a big drink, and with her mouth still wet and cold from the wine, she started kissing me.

I decided to postpone thinking about the security investigation. Lamont had given me a new assignment, and I visited my father's condo whenever I could. We sat in the bedroom together and watched late night TV. I started drinking shots of Jack Daniel's with him. He said less and less and drank more.

My mother and McIntyre had invited us for Christmas Eve dinner. McIntyre came to the door in an orange polyester shirt with the two top buttons undone, showing off his hairy chest. He wore a thick gold chain that looked rather pimp. Candles burned all over the living room with little brass angels spinning in the updraft, making tinkling sounds from all corners. After drinking eggnog laced with brandy, we listened to symphonic Christmas music while putting the last decorations on the tree. My mother seemed happy.

We sat in the living room, while McIntyre told stories about playing football in the snow as a young boy in Buffalo. Then my mother served a Christmas feast with glazed ham, mashed potatoes, baked squash, hot spiced cider, and homemade pumpkin pie. McIntyre was congenial—he smiled broadly as he gestured.

"I'm going to love your mother like no man has ever loved her," he said, winking at me.

As the evening wore on, we opened a few small gifts and played Trivial Pursuit. McIntyre chain-smoked Camels and drank glass after glass of Scotch and water.

He began making comments to Chrissie about her "beautiful white skin" and her "dynamite figure."

Then he looked at me. "Your mother hadn't had sex in years, but I took care of that. She says I'm like a pneumatic jackhammer in the sack!"

"Gordon!" she said, "It's Christmas Eve for God's sake!"

"Let's have a toast," Chrissie said with a grin. "To new experiences."

We all raised our glasses and clinked them.

"I have an announcement to make," said McIntyre, slurring his words slightly. "I'm taking your mother on a South American cruise, starting January 2nd. It's a show of my intentions. I want to marry her."

I was taken aback, but before I could react, Chrissie was ready with another toast. "To shuffleboard and skeet shooting," she said, giggling.

Then McIntyre said, "I'm going to take your father for everything I can get. Your mother deserves to be compensated for her years with that bastard."

"I can't listen to this," I said. "We should go."

Chrissie looked at me like I was crazy. She was having fun. My mother asked me to step into the bedroom.

"Give him a chance," she said. "You can see he's been drinking. He's fiercely loyal to me. I must say, it's refreshing to have a champion instead of a detractor."

"You know I'm caught in the middle. I can't take sides."

"You're absolutely right. And I love you very much. But I deserve a life too, and this is probably my last chance."

She hugged me, then we walked back into the dining room. Chrissie was laughing at something McIntyre had said. He was sitting right next to her.

On the way home, we drove along the beach esplanade. Warm dry Santa Ana winds were blowing from the east. A rare twinkling dome of stars could be seen overhead.

"You know, he's a lot more fun than your dad. He's more natural, more comfortable 'wif' himself," Chrissie said.

"This isn't the best time for that comment."

Chrissie became quiet as we drove. Then she asked me to pull over for a mineral water. We stopped at a place on the Coast Highway. Walking through the hard liquor section, she paused and slowly picked up a painted porcelain "Las Vegas Elvis" full of Jim Beam. Her hands trembled as she examined it under the strong fluorescent lights. She was transfixed, as if it were encrusted with rubies and emeralds. Suddenly it slipped and dropped to the floor. White shards of Elvis splattered on the linoleum as bourbon splashed all over us. The sweet smell of 100 proof whiskey filled the air. The clerk ran over and started yelling at us in a thick Korean accent.

"Eighty dollah! Eighty dollah! Now! Now!"

I stood there for a second without saying anything, then handed him my Visa card.

Chrissie looked dazed. "I'm sorry," she said, looking down at the mess on the floor.

She seemed to be fading as we drove. I was angry because she must have taken something at McIntyre's. She weaved unsteadily as we walked toward the elevator in the underground parking lot. Once inside the apartment, she fell onto the futon, dead to the world. The midnight bells from the Unitarian Church at the end of the block were playing "Ode to Joy." I pulled off her cowboy boots one at a time and covered her up. But I was worried she might be in trouble, so I checked her carotid pulse and her breathing. Both were strong and regular. At 4:00 am I woke up to check her again.

❈ ❈ ❈

The span between Christmas and New Year's Eve was a dead zone at HighFrontier. Many managers were on vacation, which was excellent for getting real work done. There were no useless meetings to attend or redundant memos to write. I was cleaning up some loose ends on a new telemetry processing project. Lamont came in unexpectedly and wanted to see all the code I had written. He sat behind me on his stool, breathing like a bellows, asking me questions about all the different functionalities. Finally, he said the programming looked "pretty good." But he seemed distant. Then he mentioned that the NSA were on-site again.

A call came at my desk an hour later. They wanted me to report to the same conference room. There were two agents this time inside the small white room. The guy with a moustache had returned with a smaller, older man with short gray hair—presumably the boss. They wore almost identical dark blue suits. We all shook hands and they wished me good afternoon without introducing themselves. The older one shuffled through the pages of my file, looking down the whole time. Finally, he spoke.

"Mr. Hargraves, we are upset to learn that the situation with Ms. Lundquist has not been resolved."

"That's true," I said, without offering an explanation.

"It must be resolved soon or we will have to take action. Do you understand what that means?"

"No," I said.

"Your basic clearance will be revoked," he said.

"What is the definition of soon?" I asked.

"You have until January 10th," he said

We sat and looked at each other for a few seconds.

They were completely stoic. My mind raced, evaluating the possibilities, but I said nothing. I was wondering if this was a violation of my constitutional rights.

I went to the cafeteria for a coffee. On the way back, Lamont invited me into his office and closed the door.

"Listen, I'm not supposed to breathe a word to you about the progress of a security investigation. But if I were you, I'd move her out, but go ahead and see her on the side. I don't think there's anything they can do about it. That way, you've satisfied their direct request. Give it some thought."

I nodded.

"If things continue to go well, and we can get this clearance problem behind us, I'd like to offer you a promotion to Engineering Specialist...within the next six months. That would include a significant raise."

"That sounds interesting," I said.

Lamont and I both stood up. As we shook hands, his eyes met mine. For the first time, his shields were down. I caught a flickering glimpse of the man inside.

When I got home, Chrissie was on the phone. She was starting to look like a junkie—dark circles under her eyes and blotchy complexion. I wanted her to get off the line so I could tell her she was fucking up my career at HighFrontier.

Suddenly she put down the phone. "That was Linda. Bukowski's having a big New Year's Eve party! It'll be really great. Sean Penn might come and André Broussard, the French director, will be there for sure." Then she came close and whispered, "There's also a chance that Bono might come. The band is in town and he's a big Bukowski fan. Don't tell anybody. Linda swore me to secrecy."

"I'm not getting my top-secret security clearance," I said.

"Well, you told me you weren't really interested in that. And besides, who cares about that kind of crap anyway," she said.

"I'm not getting it because of you. They think you're a drug addict and a security risk."

"I don't give a shit about your security clearance. Do you really want to work at that bomb factory for the rest of your life? You'll be bald and fat and live in a little stucco house 'wif' a crabgrass lawn. I can see it!" She grabbed her guitar case. "I'm going out to play an open mic at Sweetwater. I'll be home when I'm home," she said, slamming the door behind her.

I drew a big bathtub of steaming hot water and got down low so I could stare up at the ceiling. There were little flecks of glitter sprayed into the cottage cheese stucco. I had never noticed that before. For a long time, I sat there thinking of nothing. As I toweled off and got into bed, I decided to wait until New Year's Day to make any decisions.

In the middle of the night, I awakened with a throbbing erection. Chrissie was nude in bed next to me, I hadn't heard her come in. Her hand slipped behind my neck as I stirred. Then she began to move slowly and rhythmically, grinding against my hip as she wrapped her legs around mine. I could feel her breathing deepen; her breasts brushed my arm. As I turned my head, her lips were against mine. The room was so dark I could only catch glimpses of her white skin from the corners of my eyes. Her hands moved lightly over my chest and across my thighs as we kissed. She made slight breathy sounds as she started working my cock with one hand and delicately rubbing my stomach and thighs with the other. Then she gave me head as I caressed her back. Finally, she pulled me on top. The covers were tangled and she kicked them onto the floor. We moved slowly against each other, then together in sync, then against each other again—back and forth, in perfect rhythm. It was languid, rolling, and relaxed. She came in waves of low moaning. Afterward she snuggled close and quickly went to sleep with her arm across my chest. The next morning, I wondered if it had been a dream. I felt like we had visited another realm. We never talked about it.

The night of December 30th, I took Chrissie out to shop for clothes. She looked rejuvenated; the dark circles under her eyes had dissipated. We wandered through the giant Del Amo Mall, but she couldn't find anything that looked right. As we passed a window at Frederick's of Hollywood, I noticed a mannequin wearing a scoop backed Lycra-Spandex leopard print body suit with high heels.

"That's it," I said. "If you really want to knock 'em dead, that's what you should wear."

She looked at it and wrinkled her nose. "Don't you think it looks...trampy?"

"Let's just take a look," I said.

We stepped inside and gazed at the mannequin.

A middle-aged female salesclerk walked up behind us. "Honey, you've got the body to wear that and it won't last forever. You'd better go for it."

Chrissie hesitated, then said, "O.K. I'll try it on."

Every eye in the store followed her out of the dressing room. She was long and slinky, and it fit like skin.

"You'll burn down the house," said the clerk,

"Let's get it," I said.

Walking back toward the dressing room with her hand on her hip, she turned and winked. Then she handed me the outfit when she came out. It was about the size of a large sock.

As we walked through the mall toward the parking lot, Chrissie decided that I should buy something too. I usually wore long sleeved oxford shirts with blue jeans. But I let her pick out an Italian shirt and black slacks from a small elegant men's store. She told me I looked like a Hollywood producer.

Chrissie and I took a shower together to get ready for the party. She liked it scalding, until her skin erupted in prickly red patches. I had to get out.

Finally, as she emerged, her skin slowly reverted back to milky white with a sprinkling of pale freckles. After spraying her hair and teasing it up, she went to the closet and took out a short white faux-fur jacket.

Gazing at herself in the mirror, she smiled. The outfit looked great. I put on the Italian shirt and slacks. Then we opened a bottle of red wine.

"Let's drink to forgetting," I said, lifting my glass.

"Every-fing but tonight," she said, as our glasses came together.

On the way to San Pedro, "Fat Angel" by Donovan was on the radio. She sang along with soul, doing a harmony part.

"If I had been born at the right time, I would have been the acid queen of the Sunset Strip," she said. Then she pulled a joint out of her purse and pushed in my cigarette lighter.

Driving up the long incline toward Bukowski's, we could hear music. Cars were parked on both sides of the street all the way down the block. We walked along the dark and narrow driveway toward the front door. Chrissie rang the bell and we waited. Then she rang it again. Finally, I knocked hard. Linda came to the door smoking one of Buk's Beedis.

"Oh my God! You have got to be kidding!" She started laughing uproariously, then called people over to see Chrissie's outfit. A number of other women started laughing too. Chrissie shot an angry look at me. We stepped inside.

A man with a heavy German accent said, "I like it!"

Chrissie's face was flushed. I grabbed her arm and led her past Linda into the living room.

There were two scenes: one centered around the hors

d'oeuvres table where director Broussard was standing, and another around the long sofa and wooden table in the living room where Bukowski held court. People were perched on big pillows arranged next to the table. Chrissie and I sat down on the sofa. Buk said nothing as we arrived. He was already drunk and in the midst of a story. There were long pauses as he sucked on a Beedi. The group hung on his every word.

"I read in the downtown public library during the day, and slept in the alleys at night. Told stories in the bars to hustle drinks. Normal people bored me—I couldn't live that life, couldn't be around that. But in the end, the bums bored me too. The only thing that lasts is wine." He took a puff. "Just drink and drink...whatever else happens, is just what happens."

Bukowski's speech was slow and his eyes were like slits. He continued. "Later, I had my own room in a skid row hotel. After a particularly long night of drinking, I started puking up blood and foul-smelling chunks of flesh. It just came and came into the toilet. The stench was overpowering. They took me in an ambulance to the charity ward at County General. One of the doctors said he'd level with me—I had about a 50-50 chance. I stayed there for a month and slowly got better. When it was time to go, a doctor sat down with me in a little white room. He said if I EVER drank alcohol again, I would die." Long pause. "So, I walked out and found a shitty little bar right down the street. It smelled good—cigar smoke and stale booze. I sat down and ordered a glass of beer. No hard liquor, because I was trying to go easy. I watched the bubbles rise up, then drank it down fast." He paused and took a puff. "I didn't die."

"Amazing story!" blurted out a young guy.

"Wow," gasped a middle-aged woman. Everyone murmured with approval as they took deep pulls of wine.

Bukowski stared out the window toward the harbor. Then he turned to me. "I was wondering if you'd show up, man. I thought you might be grist for a poem if you have enough wine. So, drink up!"

He raised his glass to me. I clinked it and took a drink. Then I glanced over at Chrissie. She was scanning the room looking for rock stars and listening with one ear to André Broussard's monologue. He was saying something about the French Revolution.

A guy sitting on the other side of Bukowski said, "You're the most important writer of the late twentieth century."

Bukowski slowly turned and asked, "What do you do, kid?"

"I'm an actor," the guy said. He had a finely trimmed goatee and wore a black turtleneck with black jeans.

Bukowski paused and looked into his face, then took a drink. "You'll never make it man...your eyes are dead. There's nothing there. Give it up now, before you waste any more time. Go into insurance or real estate."

The group went silent. Bukowski took another drag from his cigarette as the guy nervously got up and walked away.

I suddenly noticed that Chrissie was standing next to Broussard, looking at him adoringly. Sean Penn and Bono hadn't shown up, so Broussard was the biggest fish in the house. As I got up and walked past that group on my way to the kitchen, Broussard was telling Chrissie a story about the Marquis de Sade.

"The Marquis whipped the people into a frenzy, with political rants and kinky sex monologues." I saw him glance at her chest. Then I heard him say, "I like your outfit. It's very chic. I think you are making your own fashion statement."

I sat back down on the sofa next to Bukowski.

"I'm glad you're here, man," he said. "I need somebody with a brain sitting next to me."

He stared at me, waiting for a response. I took a drink. The crowd around the sofa had thinned out since the encounter with the actor. Nobody wanted to get too close. Linda came over and sat on the floor next to Buk, with her legs crossed in a semi-lotus pose. Long strawberry blond hair flowed halfway down her back. She lit up a joint.

"I've got my own rock 'n' roll groupie," he said. "She parties all night in the brand-new convertible I bought her. And I don't even ask who she's fucking. Do I?"

"This is not the time," she said, taking a drag from the joint. The muscles in her jaw tightened.

"You've been riding my coat-tails for years. If it wasn't for me, where the hell would you be?"

"I have no idea," she said. The room was silent.

Linda's eyes blazed with anger.

"I think you're being too hard on her," I said.

"I think you'd better shut up, motherfuck. You haven't been very entertaining tonight. In fact, you're beginning to bore me," he said, moving his face close to mine. His eyes were mean and glassy, like a vicious animal.

As he got up to go to the bathroom, he reeled and started to lose his balance. I reached up to steady him, but he swatted my hand away. Then he staggered across the room and disappeared into the bathroom. A group of Linda's friends from the health food restaurant stood near the bathroom talking about how much they liked John Tesh's music. Suddenly the bathroom door flew open. Bukowski emerged and walked quickly toward a balding man in a cardigan sweater.

"Where's your drink?!" Bukowski demanded.

"This is my drink," said the man, holding up a Calistoga water.

Bukowski turned to a woman nearby, "Where's your drink?"

"I don't drink," the woman cheerfully replied.

Bukowski went nose-to-nose with her and said, "Then get out! You bore me!" He turned to the man and said, "You get out, too!" Then he looked around the room and shouted, "In fact, I want everybody out. I should be upstairs typing. I might die tomorrow and I DON'T want to spend my last night on earth with this bunch!" He started walking around the room screaming in people's faces, "GET OUT! GET OUT! GET THE FUCK OUT OF MY HOUSE!"

People quickly gathered up their purses and coats. Most looked afraid as they headed toward the front door. Bukowski continued to scream, "GET OUT, GET OUT!" The arteries on his neck bulged and his face had turned purple. He planted his hand on various backs—male or female—and pushed them out the door. Linda watched in silence, still seething with anger. Bukowski stood guard until the last stragglers had gone. As I left, I looked over my shoulder, but there was no hint of recognition.

I walked slowly down the long driveway and scanned the crowd. Chrissie was missing. When I got to the sidewalk, three men in their early twenties were craning their necks trying to look inside the house.

"What is happening? What is happening?" one asked, with a German accent.

"Bukowski threw everybody out...because we weren't drinking enough."

"This is very cool," he said. "Very Bukowski!"

"We've come all the way from Munich to meet him!" said another guy.

"It's a bad night to ring the doorbell," I said. "He'll tear your head off."

"We saw André Broussard!" he added. "Got his autograph as he was leaving in a limousine with a nice prostitute." Then he smiled, "I'm sure he got a blowjob as soon as they were inside."

My throat knotted up.

I got into my Citroën a few minutes before the stroke of midnight. Skyrockets whizzed into the darkness. Gunshots erupted from the neighborhoods at the bottom of the hill. Rounds were going off in all directions. Suddenly I heard the buzz-and-zing of a nearby bullet.

Driving aimlessly, I screeched around corners and floored the accelerator, almost hoping the engine would blow. When I got home, the message light was on. I thought it would be Chrissie with some bullshit story about where she was. Then I recognized my mother's voice. She was sobbing uncontrollably.

"It was...almost midnight. One more day...and we would have been gone on our cruise. Just one more day!" She gasped for breath. Then the message ended.

McIntyre and my mother had stepped onto the balcony of the Jonathan Beach Club for some fresh air. He lit a cigarette as they gazed out at the sweeping arc of lights spanning toward Palos Verdes Estates.

"I'm so happy tonight, being here with you," he said, turning to look at her.

She hesitated for a moment, then turned toward him. They kissed.

He looked at his watch. "It's nearly midnight. I'll get some Champagne."

My mother stared at the towering Christmas tree

covered in fairy lights and hundreds of ornaments. It reminded her of New York City, when she was a young woman.

She made eye contact with McIntyre as he left the bar. Smiling broadly, he walked toward her. Then his expression suddenly changed, and his eyes widened. He abruptly stopped as his face became a twisted mask of pain. The glasses dropped to the floor. Clutching his chest, he staggered, then fell to his knees.

"My God! Somebody help! My God!" she screamed as she ran into the ballroom.

I called my father. He said that McIntyre was dead on arrival at the emergency room at St. John's in Santa Monica. My mother had ridden in the ambulance. Then she called my father and he picked her up at the hospital.

"She's here with me now." He sounded more himself than he had in months. I could hear her crying in the background. "I have to go," he said.

I turned on the TV. It was a replay of the ball drop in Times Square. Counting, 5-4-3-2-1...then explosive crowd noise. Happy New Year. I cracked open a beer and turned on my computer to write an email to Lamont. But in the middle, I deleted it. Instead, I started writing a story. By 3:45 am, I had knocked out seven pages rapid fire. I had the machinegun rhythms of Bukowski's black Underwood in my head. Then the telephone rang. It was Chrissie. Her voice sounded faint. She was in the lobby of the Château Marmont hotel.

"Broussard said he was going to put me in a movie. How stupid could I be? He's a drunk and a bore and an asshole. You're the only one who really gets me. I love you. Will you let me come back?"

I paused, "Yeah, come back. We're going to hit the road—Prague, Morocco, India, who knows where? Are you ready for that?"

"Cool," she said without hesitating. "I'm there."

Michael D. Meloan's fiction has appeared in *Wired, Huffington Post, Buzz, LA Weekly, Larry Flynt's Chic,* and in many anthologies. He was an interview subject in the documentaries *Bukowski: Born Into This* and *Joe Frank: Somewhere Out There.* With Joe Frank, he co-wrote a number of radio shows that aired across the National Public Radio syndicate. His *Wired* short story "The Cutting Edge" was optioned for film. And he co-authored the novel *The Shroud* with his brother Steven. For many years, he was a software engineer. In addition, he does killer karaoke.